The Tinderbox

the tinderbox

A Novel by Marianne Brandis

with original wood engravings
by G. Brender à Brandis

The Porcupine's Quill, 1982

Published by The Porcupine's Quill, 68 Main Street, Erin, Ontario NOB 1TO. Financial assistance towards publication was gratefully received by both author and publisher from the Canada Council and the Ontario Arts Council.

Distributed by Firefly Books, 3520 Pharmacy Avenue, Unit 1C, Scarborough, Ontario M1W 2T8.

Printed and bound in June of 1982 by The Porcupine's Quill, Inc. The type is Palatino, composed at Howarth & Smith (Toronto), and the stock is Zephyr laid.

Signed prints of many of these engravings may be purchased from the artist at The Brandstead Press, Carlisle, Ontario LOR 1HO.

ISBN 0-88984-064-4 (paper)
      0-88984-076-8 (case)

Except for Mr. Lesslie, the characters who appear in this novel are imaginary. The setting depicts, as far as we have found possible, a specific region of Upper Canada as it was in 1830.

We wish to thank Janet Black, Ernie Harrison, Roberta M. Styran, Mrs. Jean Hughes of Black Creek Pioneer Village, and the staff of Wentworth Pioneer Village.

CHAPTER ONE

Flames are very bright at night, and their light seems to spill out over the snow like red liquid. As Emma watched her family's house burn, one part of her mind was observing the colours and the towering pillar of sparks and smoke, rising straight up towards the sky from which some ashes and a few snowflakes fell. The rest of her attention was concentrated on the door of the house from which her parents and the small children should be emerging. It seemed a long time but it couldn't be more than a minute or two since her father had shouted her awake, pulling her and John out of bed and shoving them down the stairs.

'Get out, Emma! Get away from the house! Look after John!'

She must have pulled on shoes and a shawl automatically; John had come barefoot and now his feet were bundled in the shawl. Where they stood, the snow had not yet been melted by the fire. It was a very cold night in March.

With horrified intensity, but able to do no more than what her father had commanded, Emma watched the fire. After a few moments, she heard steps crunching on the snowy driveway behind her. It was Mr. Wilbur from across the road, coming up at an ungainly half-run. 'I was in the barn with a sheep lambing,' he puffed. 'I've sent Dave to the Bateses. You kids stay right here.'

He took off his coat and hung it around the two children, then took a few steps towards the burning house.

Suddenly at the gaping door, bulking dark against the smoke and the flame behind him, appeared Emma's father. Emma saw him fill his lungs with air. His clothes were on fire and she was about to run to him when he turned and plunged indoors again. A second later, the roof crashed down with a roar and a soaring stream of flame.

'Let go my hand, Emma, you're hurting me.'

She had forgotten John. Now she gathered him against her, burying his face against her nightdress. She herself could not look away from the fire. Her father and mother and the two little girls were in there. She would never again see them alive. Emma was thirteen years old; not only John but also the mem-

FIREPLACE

ories of her parents and little sisters were now to be her responsibility.

Soon after the collapse of the roof, several other neighbours arrived. They stood silent, all watching the fire. Only Arnold Bates, who was a bit simple, ran back and forth between the creek and the burning house, flinging buckets of water at the blaze. No one helped him. It was a tableau which would be fixed in Emma's mind for the rest of her life: the roaring inferno with its plume of sparks and smoke, the silent people, and Arnold Bates' futile scurrying, all fused with the image of her father in the fiery doorway, gulping for air.

The fire settled down to a steady, methodical consumption of the whole log house. There was no wind and therefore no danger to the barn — where the livestock could be safely left until the next day — or to the small shanty where the Andersons had lived before they built the house. Until the fire burned itself out no one would be able to go in and get the bodies. So the people trailed away home, the Bates family to their two sprawling farms just up the road and the Wilburs to theirs directly across from the burning house. Emma and John were taken to the Wilburs' house, where their feet were rubbed back to life and they were given hot milk to drink.

'I guess we can keep 'em for a time, Liza?' asked Jake Wilbur of his wife.

'O'course we can, the poor little things.'

'Any relatives that you know of?'

'We can ask Emma tomorrow. Or Granny might know, seeing as she was so friendly with Mrs. Anderson. But I never heard tell of none.'

In the Wilburs' large kitchen stood a bed where Aggie, the oldest daughter, slept. Emma and John were put into it with Aggie; the other Wilbur children went up to the attic and Jake and Liza took the candle to their bedroom next door to the kitchen. The house became quiet. Emma wrapped her arms around John; he went to sleep at once, but she lay with open eyes, watching. Through the bare trees, and glimmering into the kitchen, came the glow of the fire.

Eventually the redness dimmed into the cold white morning light. Emma extricated herself from John's sinewy, boy-smelling body and got out of bed. She slipped into her shoes and gathered up the shawl which she had saved from the fire. The kitchen was cold, though a tiny vein of smoke pulsed up from

9

the heaped ashes on the hearth. Outdoors it would be even colder. She hesitated a moment, realizing that she had no other clothes to put on, then took the top quilt off the bed and wrapped it around herself along with the shawl.

When she looked up after tying the corners of the shawl and the quilt together, she gasped. A white form stood in the dim kitchen looking at her.

'Where're you going, Emma?'

It was Granny Wilbur, prevented by a bad cold from attending the fire during the night but clearly planning to start the work of the household as she did every morning.

'To our house. I must see . . . .' Emma turned away and went quickly to the door.

'Emma. No.'

The girl paused with her hand on the latch. The old voice was firm and quiet — both of them spoke softly so as not to wake Aggie and John.

'I must go . . . .'

'D'you know what you'll see there, Emma? Have you thought about it?'

'My mother and father, and Charlotte and Jane. Someone's got to do something for them now that the fire's out.'

'The men will go later, after the morning chores, and do what's fitting. Wait until they've . . . .'

Emma turned sharply. 'They *burned* to death, Granny. My family burned to death and everyone went home to bed.'

'Yes, child. I know it's hard. And you've been laying awake picturing it. But there's no call for you to see . . . .'

'I can't *bear* to think of them lying there in the cold — after all that heat . . . .' Emma began to cry painful tears, covering her face with her hands for privacy.

Granny led her to the bench alongside the table. After a few minutes, with visible effort, the girl calmed a little.

'Now, child, you've got to remember that the spirits of the dead have gone to a better place.'

'Do you really believe that?'

'There, you've just given me another proof that all children are little heathens. O'course I believe it.'

'But. . . .'

'Due respect'll be paid to the dead.'

'*After* the chores,' Emma said bitterly.

'Living animals and people're more important than dead

ones,' said the old woman calmly. 'That's just common sense. Now, you get that fire burning proper while I fetch down the tea-caddy.'

Emma stared. '*Fire* . . . ?' Her face began to crumple again.

Granny Wilbur took her by both hands. 'The fire on the *hearth*, girl.'

'I can't.'

'You can and you will. Take off that there quilt — you'll be warm soon enough. The kindling and bellows are right handy.'

Fearfully, but knowing somehow that the old woman was right, Emma knelt and coaxed the fire on the hearth into life.

* * *

Later that morning, dressed in borrowed clothes and with a heavy lump of grief in her heart, she watched the men carrying the bodies of her parents and little sisters out of the still-smoking ruins. Makeshift stretchers had been hammered together and bedsheets brought to cover the corpses.

Normally the dead would have been put in someone's parlour, but no one had a parlour big enough for four bodies — and besides, the ground was frozen too hard to permit the graves to be dug. 'Put 'em in that there shanty,' said Isaac Bates, pointing to the Andersons' small log cabin. 'They won't be in nobody's way and'll keep cold till we can make coffins and dig the graves and send for preacher.'

'Ground'll be frozen solid like rock,' said Arnold Bates.

'Shanty in pretty good shape, Emma?' asked Mr. Wilbur.

'Yes, a traveller stayed there last fall. Only . . . .'

'Well, then, what is it?'

'I'd just like to sweep the floor and make it nice.'

'Sure, lass, run to our house and fetch a broom.'

She swept the floor before they brought in the covered stretchers; after they left, she wiped clean the tiny window and laid a fire. The fire would not be lit, of course, because the bodies were supposed to stay frozen until they could be buried, but still the neat structure of bark and kindling looked right. She also brought in a few small evergreen boughs, the only available vegetation, to put on the sheeted forms.

Before leaving, Emma stood beside the four stretchers, laid on the floor side by side. The cold in the cabin was intense and the scent of evergreens and burned flesh hung heavily on it.

She knelt down. The lump of despair and desolation inside her rose so as almost to choke her. Here, and in the blackened ruin a few yards away, lay her childhood, her whole being. Without tears, and without understanding it fully, she contemplated the fact. She paid her personal farewell to her family and then went out, carefully closing the door behind her.

* * *

For the remainder of that day Emma wandered about, restless and lost. She stood beside the creek at the point where fast-flowing water showed black between the ice. She walked a short distance into the woods until the deep and unregarding silence frightened her out again. Towards the end of the afternoon, half numb with grief and cold, she came to stand beside the burnt-out wreck of the only home she had ever known. There was almost no smoke anymore; the few snowflakes falling idly out of a grey sky were beginning to make little white mounds and ridges on the black ruins.

She stepped over a log into what had been the house and, stooping and clambering, began searching for anything which might have survived the fire. The first thing she found was the pewter candlestick, deformed by the heat and no longer usable. She stood holding it for a moment, thinking how hideous it was now, and then dropped it. She came upon part of the leather cover of one of her father's books; it fell to pieces in her hands, leaving soot on her fingers, and she gave one choked sob as she wiped the dirt off with her handkerchief.

Under the ruins there might be other objects, but Emma did not have the strength to shift the charred logs nor the heart to sift through the ashes. She picked her way along slowly, careful not to fall into the cellar hole and not to get too much dirt on the borrowed and alien clothes.

In the middle of the wreckage there was a partly cleared patch. Here, Mr. Wilbur had told her that morning, the men had removed parts of the collapsed roof and upper floor. They had found the four bodies lying in a huddle at the foot of the steep stairs. No one had understood why Martin Anderson and his wife and small children had not been able to reach the door.

Emma stood for a while beside the cleared area, but even

12

this place meant less to her now than did the shanty with its solemn contents. She looked around, noting where the kitchen dresser had been and where her mother's chair had always stood, near the fireplace in a draught-free corner. Over there, against the inside wall away from possible dampness, had hung the bookshelf with her father's seventeen precious books on it. Here used to stand the big table which had served as kitchen counter, desk, dining table, and centre of most of the family's indoor activities. At that table her father had taught her to write and read and cipher. He had also given lessons to the other children in the little settlement — Wilburs and Bateses — but it was the evenings alone with her parents that Emma cherished, when her mother would be sewing by the fire and her father reading or talking or mending harness. Being the oldest, Emma was always allowed to stay up a bit longer than the younger children; it was a margin of seniority which she valued.

She shook her head to free it of memories which were at this moment so heartbreaking. Moving slowly, she made her way onwards until, near the far side of the wrecked house, she saw something familiar. Half-buried in ashes lay her father's tinderbox. She knelt and picked it up. It was dirty but apparently intact except for the candle-socket which ought to have been fixed on its lid. Emma poked among the soft pale ashes and, against expectation, found the candle-socket. She held it against the lid of the box where it belonged; it had been slightly loose ever since she could remember, and her father had often said that the next time he went to Waterdown he would have the blacksmith repair it.

She opened the tinderbox. The bit of flint was still there, and the piece of metal file from which the spark was struck, and the flat inner lid for extinguishing the fire when it was no longer needed. But the fragment of linen which would have served as tinder at the next time of using had been scorched to a black crisp.

The tinderbox! Out of this came the original spark which led to the past night's dreadful fire. Her first impulse was to smash it or bury it beyond recovery. But as she slowly stood up, she remembered the tinderbox in its more kindly role, producing a spark on a cold morning when the fire had gone out, or standing on table or window sill holding up a candle. In a flash she recalled that during the evening before the fire — last

13

night, in fact! — it had been standing on the window sill. That had probably saved it; it had been spared the worst of the heat and the falling of the heaviest logs.

Emma put the candle-socket inside the tinderbox and the box itself into the pocket of her borrowed dress. It was a sort of legacy, something to remember her parents by, the only object which in later years would connect her directly with them.

As she turned away, thinking that for politeness' sake she ought to go to the Wilburs, she spotted something caught under a beam. The beam was impossible to move but she dug the object out from underneath. It was her mother's silver brooch, blackened and reduced to a shapeless lump of metal. Emma wiped it with a corner of her shawl and pressed it to her face — and then with a cry she flung it away. It was cold and ugly, and it was not her mother's brooch anymore! The hideous, distorted thing was nothing like the graceful twist of filigree which her mother had worn on the front of her dress every day. Emma's mind flashed to the dead bodies, also cold and distorted, lying in the shanty. That morning, when they had been placed there, she had not had the courage to look under the sheets, but now she climbed out of the ruined house and ran to atone for that cowardice.

When she reached the shanty door, however, she paused. The bodies would be ugly and repulsive; was it really necessary to remember her parents and little sisters as they looked *now*?

But was she perhaps being disloyal, unloving, to turn away from them at this grim time?

She did not know, and there was no one to ask, no one who could advise her. The frantic sense of loss and grief swept over her again; she rested her head against the shanty door and wept fearfully.

Only when she realized that the snow was falling more heavily and that it was getting dark did she sniff hard and begin walking towards the Wilbur house. Her cold and exhausted body stumbled stupidly. The Wilburs' house would be warm, but it would not give her the kind of comfort that she needed. And how would she ever learn to live with strangers — with *strangers* — for the rest of her life?

CHAPTER TWO

Six months later, Emma and John were still living with the Wilburs. They seemed to be thoroughly at home there — especially John, who worked and played with the two half-grown Wilbur boys and showed no outward sign of missing his parents, though he still had occasional nightmares about the fire.

Emma, on the other hand, did not feel herself to be a part of the Wilbur family. Although she willingly did her share of the work in the house and barn and fields, she thought almost continuously about her parents. Her life had stopped six months ago; she had learned nothing since then except how to live with sorrow, and she seemed to have no future. The hope chest which, under her mother's guidance, she had been making against her almost inevitable marriage, had been destroyed in the fire; so had everything else that might have pointed the way to the adult life which, since her fourteenth birthday in the August of that summer, was so close but so completely blank and unimaginable.

On a warm day in late September, Emma was setting the table for mid-day dinner. Mr. Wilbur, his two sons, his daughter Bess, and Emma's brother John were harvesting potatoes. Mrs. Wilbur was stirring the stew which was the Wilburs' most usual dinner dish, and Mary, the youngest Wilbur child, was sweeping the parlour. Aggie, the oldest, had married in the course of the summer and Granny had had another of her attacks and was now bedridden. Since these last two events, Emma had become Mrs. Wilbur's main help in the house.

'You wanna take Granny her dinner before the others come?' Mrs. Wilbur asked Emma. 'Fetch a plate and I'll dish some up for her.'

Emma had a tray ready. She carried it to the fireplace, where Mrs. Wilbur spooned stew onto the plate while Emma filled the cup with herb tea from the pot which stood all day on a hob by the fire. As she added milk to the tea, she heard the potato harvesters arrive in the yard, and in a moment they filled the kitchen with their big outdoor voices.

'I picked the most potatoes!' Ted shouted.

'No, me!' clamoured David.

'Shut up, the both of you,' Mr. Wilbur commanded, but the argument went on.

'Can I drive the horse after, when we bring the load in?' John asked.

Trust John to want to work with the horse, Emma thought. This summer horses had become his chief interest in life.

'Bess, you didn't fetch me no water from the creek this morning,' Mrs. Wilbur said. 'You'll just have to do it after dinner, 'fore you go back to the field.'

'Aw, can't Mary or Emma do it?'

'Well, maybe. I'll see.' Mrs. Wilbur was an easy-going woman, kindly enough but soft in every way. She had little insight or understanding and Emma was surprised that she managed to create even a small degree of order in the house. The girl often compared the Wilbur style of housekeeping to the much more orderly one which she had been learning from her mother. Then, thinking of the Wilburs' kindness to herself and John, she was ashamed.

Granny's room was on the ground floor, beyond the one in which Mr. and Mrs. Wilbur slept. It was a small but tranquil place. Emma, having put the tray on the old lady's lap, sat down for a moment on the edge of the chair. She should go back to the kitchen and eat her dinner, but this room was now the nearest thing she had to a home. The shanty where the bodies of her family had lain was her other special place but it was more a shrine than a home.

'Well, Emma, what are your plans for this afternoon?' Granny asked.

'Mrs. Wilbur wants me to pick the grapes on our place. The wild grapes at the top of the field, remember?'

'What's she going to do with them?'

'Make wine, I guess.'

'Hmphm! 'Twon't be a patch on yer ma's wine. I remember well. . . .' The old lady sank into silence, staring out beyond the foot of her bed.

A surge of loneliness swept over Emma. All the Wilburs talked as though Emma's parents had existed in some distant, legendary time. Even Granny, who had been closest to them! This attitude made the emptiness around Emma so much more bleak, her life so much more solitary. Emma's wounds were still raw; but it seemed as though no one else (except perhaps John) felt anything at all.

A restless movement from the bed recalled Emma's attention. 'Well,' announced Granny, with a glance at the girl, 'no use talking about wine when there's lots more important things we miss yer ma 'n' pa for.' With an angry thump, she brought her hand down on the Bible which lay beside her. 'It ain't right that they should've been taken. It just ain't right.'

The words gave Emma a grain of comfort but did not really satisfy her. While the old lady ate a few spoonfuls of stew, Emma reflected that no one had known her parents as she had done. And only in that last winter, during the long evenings, had Emma herself begun to see them as people rather than merely as parents. They had treated her as an adult and Emma had come to realize that her father was not merely well-educated and a born teacher, but that he was truly learned and wise as well. As a result of an injury received when fighting the Americans in 1813, his left arm was weak and often painful. He made up for this handicap by using his mind.

His wife had her own wisdom, mainly a wisdom about people. Though she was a good housekeeper, she had little in common with most farm women. She had, however, made friends with Granny Wilbur, whose father had been a schoolmaster in Massachusetts before the American War of Independence and who talked about subjects other than crops and sicknesses.

Emma had felt, this summer, as though she had inherited Granny from her mother. Perhaps that was why it was so sad that Granny did not fully share her grief.

'Them wild grape vines,' Granny said, after drinking some tea. 'Funny there should be just that one patch of them, on yer pa's farm. If they'd have been on this place, nobody'd have recognized them and they would've been pulled right out.'

'Father explained why they grew there,' Emma began, and then her voice failed. She saw him again, as vivid as though she could touch the solid reality of him, explaining about the south-facing slope, with the woods behind to shelter the grapes from the cold winds. That was what grapevines liked, just as in France, where a lot of wine was made. He was good at explaining things, pointing out the wood-grain in the end of a log or the structure of a bird's nest. On winter afternoons at the long table in the Andersons' house, he had taught all the children on the four farms — his contribution to the little community in place of the heavy work which, with his bad arm, he was unable to do. He had owned a copy of Mavor's *Spelling Book*, and Granny Wilbur had contributed a *New England Primer* inherited from her father. With these, and the Bible, and half a dozen frayed copies of the *Colonial Advocate*, and two volumes from a much larger set of *The Spectator*, he had taught the children to read. On a slate, used turn and turn about, they had learned the beginnings of writing and ciphering. Inside the back cover of the *Spelling Book*, he had drawn a map of Upper Canada on which he had pointed out where the main battles of the recent war against the Americans had taken place. But he was not a war-loving man and talked more readily about the ships on the lakes, and the town of York where he had lived for a time, and the great St. Lawrence River which flowed past Montreal and Quebec to the ocean.

Emma roused herself and stood up. 'Time I went to have my dinner,' she said.

'You can take this back,' Granny said, touching the tray with one bent and bony forefinger.

'You haven't eaten much, Granny.'

'What's left'll go back in the pot. I don't need much, lying here all day. I don't want to get fat.' All her wrinkles smiled. It was a standing joke, because Granny had always been thin and, in the last months, seemed to have become even thinner.

Emma was leaning over to pick up the tray when Granny spoke again. 'Before you go, girl, give me a kiss.'

Emma put the tray aside, embraced the old lady, and then sat on the edge of the bed for a moment, holding both her hands. Granny was so very old and frail — and, at the realization, Emma shivered slightly. 'I'll bring you some grapes when I get back.'

'Wear your hat when you're outside, and don't get your nose sunburnt.'

* * *

After dinner, Emma set off to pick the grapes. She put on the wide-brimmed hat — bought in June from the peddler's cart — that she wore outdoors to protect her skin. Wearing the hat, she looked older than her fourteen years. During the summer she had grown tall and had just begun to fill out, revealing the sort of woman she would become. Her hair had always been an acorn-coloured, stubborn bush, hanging in a single thick braid down her back except for the fluff of uncontrollable short hairs about her face. Her skin had something of the redhead's pallor and fineness. The dress she wore — donated by Aggie Wilbur after the fire — was old and faded and too short, exposing shabby boots that had belonged to one of the Bates women.

In the open-sided shed just outside the back door, she picked up two baskets and the garden shears. She had just set off down the driveway when she heard a shout.

'Hey, Emma!'

She stopped and turned, blinking into the sunlight. Beside the barn, where she hadn't noticed him, was Isaac Bates, apparently about to mount to the seat of his one-horse cart.

'Oh, hello, Isaac.'

Instead of climbing onto the cart, he came walking towards her, leading the horse by its bridle. He was one of the Bates clan which lived just up the road on two adjoining farms. Isaac was twenty-four, a stocky man, black-haired and deeply tanned after a whole summer of working outdoors. He was unmarried and still lived and worked on his father's farm but would very soon be moving to land of his own.

'Goin' up the road?' he asked. 'Give you a ride, if you like.'

'No, thanks. I'm only going across to our place to pick grapes.'

'Grapes, eh?' He gave her a sidelong look as they walked down the driveway.

'I thought you'd be busy with the harvesting, Isaac.'

'So I am. Came to borrow a shovel and some baskets.' He scratched the thicket of hair that showed in the open collar of his shirt. 'Fine day for harvestin'.'

'Yes, it is. How do your crops look?'

'Great. Just great.'

'Mr. Wilbur and the boys and Bess are getting the potatoes in today.'

'Yeah, I know, I talked to Jake over the fence.'

They reached the road, where he would turn left and she right. She made a move to go on her way but he didn't. 'Say, Emma, how're you makin' out? I mean. . . .'

She looked at him, a little puzzled. Right after the fire, everyone had been concerned about the plight of the orphans

BASKETS

but lately the assumption seemed to be that they would stay with the Wilburs until they were old enough to marry or move away on their own. Emma was not at all sure what Isaac's question meant; there was something uncharacteristically vague about it.

'Oh, all right, I guess,' she said hesitantly.

He looked at her squarely, not with his usual raking, sideways glance. His eyes rested first on her face, and their expression was serious and thoughtful. Emma realized with an inward quiver of pleasure and nervousness that he was regarding her as an adult, not as a child. She met his look for a moment and watched as his expression changed from thoughtfulness to something questioning, demanding, almost devouring. Then the touch of his eyes slid down her body and she quickly bent her head so that hat-brim shielded her face.

'Well, g'day to you, then,' he said, as though he had received a satisfactory answer.

She looked up in time to see him climb onto the cart; he clucked the horse into motion and the cart went off bumping and rattling.

Emma walked along the road a few yards and then turned into the driveway of the place that she still considered home. But for once her mind was not full of grief and the memory of the fire. Isaac's glance down her body had reminded her of something else — a comment she had overheard, about a year ago, when she went to look for her father in the barn. Isaac had been with him, helping with some heavy work, and as Emma came suddenly upon them she heard her father say, 'Never trust a woman who wears stays, Isaac.' Emma knew what stays were — her mother had described them but didn't wear them herself because they interfered with hard work. They sounded very uncomfortable. Emma, standing invisible just inside the barn, had wondered what on earth could have led the two men to talk about women wearing stays. Isaac had laughed in a strange way and Emma, when she stepped into view, had seen a look in his eyes which was like the one she had seen just now, though on that occasion it had been directed not at her but at some inward mental picture. Her father, when he had turned to her, wore his whimsical face. She never did learn what they had been talking about.

Now she wondered, more than she had on that other occasion, what that look meant and why, just now, he had di-

GRAPES OVER SUMAC

rected it towards her. Though it made her uncomfortable, she had almost enjoyed it; she did like being treated as an adult.

*　*　*

The driveway was overgrown with weeds and grass. This summer it had been used only by Mr. Wilbur who had mowed the hay in one of the Anderson fields and carted it to his own barn. 'No sense wasting it,' he had said, and Emma agreed completely. On her left was the ruined house with her mother's little garden next to it and the barn behind it, further back from the road. On her right was the shanty where the Andersons had lived until the house was built and where the bodies had lain for six weeks, waiting until the ground thawed enough to enable the men to dig graves. To Emma the shanty was sacred, as though it were still occupied by the spirits of the dead. When she thought of them, this was to her the significant place, not the Wilburs' little graveyard where they were buried. She seldom visited the graves, but she came here often.

She had no time to stop there now. Instead she went on, past the barn and into the sloping field at the top of which the grapes grew. The field was thick with grass and weeds which dragged at Emma's dress and brushed the bottoms of the baskets. Isaac Bates and two of his brothers had helped Martin Anderson clear this field. It was in return for such assistance that he had taught the Bates and Wilbur children to read and write and cipher.

The slope had been cleared up to where the grapes were; the vines grew at the boundary between field and forest, twisting themselves around saplings, bushes, a fallen beech tree, and some stumps which had been dragged to this spot after the clearing of the field.

When she reached the place, Emma put down the baskets and sat on a large rock for a moment. The drowsy heat, so good for ripening grapes, weighed on her until she felt almost dizzy. She ate a few grapes, rich-tasting and nourishing. Then she took off her hat and, while using it to fan her face, looked back over the shallow valley with the brush-fringed stream winding through it to touch all four farms in turn — the two Bates homesteads off to the right, the Wilburs', and the Andersons' directly below her.

She could see Mr. Wilbur and the four young people gathering potatoes; beyond the field where they worked was another one in which some of the Bates people were doing the same. None of the pumpkins had been harvested yet — Emma could see the orange specks among the stumps in several of the partly cleared areas. On the far slope of the valley, and slightly misted by the thick autumn air, one of the Bates men was ploughing with a team of oxen, raising a slowly-drifting cloud of dust as he went.

Then a glimpse of movement closer by caught her attention. To the left, at the edge of the forest that separated this group of farms from the settled land near Waterdown, another cloud of dust appeared. Whatever was making it was hidden by the woods along the creek. It must be a visitor, because all the Wilburs and Bateses were home. Emma watched until it reappeared, splashing across the creek at the ford: it was a buckboard, and on the seat beside the driver sat a lady!

Emma stared. The buckboard disappeared behind a clump of trees. When it came in sight again it was nearer, and Emma studied the lady as well as she could from that distance. She was wearing a black dress, and her face was hidden by a wide hat with ruffles on the brim. The hands were gloved and clasped together. And the lady was sitting very erect and stiff, in spite of the jolting of the buckboard.

A wave of uneasiness washed over Emma. For a moment she couldn't understand it, and then she remembered. Last year — it must be almost exactly a year ago — she had been up here picking grapes when, happening to look down the slope, she had seen a man standing at the door of the house. A peddler's pack lay at his feet but he was not their usual peddler — a friendly young man who had lately exchanged his pack for a small cart. This man was dressed in black and was talking to Emma's mother. Emma had felt a sudden chill of uneasiness as though the strange peddler had brought danger or bad news. Remembering that her father was away in Waterdown and her mother alone with John and the two little girls, Emma had run down the hill to help in case of need. When she reached the house the man had just taken his leave. Emma and her mother had watched him walk down the driveway, and Anne Anderson had said, 'He wasn't a peddler, I'm sure of that. Maybe he was spying about, seeing what belongings we had or . . . or something.' When Emma had mentioned her uneasiness, her mother had looked at her curiously and explained that there were some people who saw or sensed things that others didn't. Emma could not remember the exact word her mother had used, but that was what it had meant.

And now she felt that same chill of uneasiness, even though this visitor was a lady of very respectable appearance.

The buckboard turned in at the Wilburs' driveway and disappeared behind the house; when it came into view again the lady was not on it. Emma, seeing the driver more clearly, recognized him as the hostler from the inn in Waterdown. The lady could, therefore, be from Waterdown itself. But through that village travelled the coaches that connected York and Dundas and all the world beyond, so the visitor might have come from anywhere.

The thought of Dundas reminded Emma that Granny had lived there before coming here. Perhaps the lady was a friend of hers who had come for a visit. And with a small lifting of the spirits, Emma hoped that the visitor — one of the very few to come to this isolated settlement — might have brought a book or newspaper with her.

The buckboard vanished into the woods towards Waterdown, and Emma turned to the grapes. It was a good crop, and she was pleased to see how quickly the first basket was filled. The second took longer because she had to reach higher, climb on stumps or the fallen tree, and carefully pull down the vines to cut the bunches of grapes. But at length it too was full.

As she took a moment's rest she thought, with another little tremor of uneasiness, of the visitor in the black dress. She realized that she would have to meet the lady, and for the first time in a long while she was aware of her borrowed clothes, so shabby and ill-fitting. She hated to be introduced to a stranger when she looked like this. As she absent-mindedly tugged at the waist of her dress, she remembered Isaac again and blushed.

To shake off these thoughts, and to get the grapes away from a dozen wasps which had gathered about them, she picked up the baskets and set off down the slope. Mrs. Wilbur would be glad of such a lot of grapes — though, like Granny, Emma was not at all sure that the resulting wine would be as good as Anne Anderson's. Of course Mrs. Wilbur was expecting Emma to remember how her mother made wine. But the

ABANDONED GARDEN

recipe, if there had ever been one, had perished in the fire, and Emma was not sure that she could recall enough of it to justify Mrs. Wilbur's touching confidence in her memory and abilities.

When she reached the burned house she put down the heavy baskets to rest her arms and walked over to the ruin. It had produced a magnificent crop of fireweed whose empty seed-pods still hung on the tall, coarse stalks. A small snake slid off a beam where it had been sunning itself. Emma went to the remains of her mother's kitchen garden. In the spring she had resolved that she would keep the garden going but she had after all not had the time for it. She had, however, picked the strawberries and rhubarb which had grown even without attention, and now she was looking for some squashes which she had seen earlier in the summer growing on a plant which had evidently seeded itself. She found only what was left of them — an animal had eaten most of each one. And as she stood there, the half-eaten squashes making her disproportionately sad, she remembered her mother in the garden, squatting down to tuck seeds into the ground or to pick things from low plants, or bending to see what small Charlotte or Jane was putting into her mouth, or pointing out a head of lettuce which had been nibbled by a deer. She had been a beautiful woman, tall and slim and with an expressive body. Emma realized in a flash how attractive she must have been to men — and perhaps to everybody.

Then she thought of the rigid form of the lady on the buckboard, a form too stiff, by the look of it, ever to bend in that way. 'Never trust a woman who wears stays!' It had been spoken lightly, but Emma knew how serious some jokes could be. Her disquiet increased again.

As she turned away from the garden, back to the burned house and the baskets of grapes, Emma saw again in her mind's eye the fire. She flinched and covered her eyes for a moment, and the grief at the loss of her parents gripped her again. She stood still for a moment, then dropped her hands and stared at the shanty. There seemed no end to the sorrow and the remembering; her present life was not interesting enough to absorb her mind, and its shapelessness compared badly with the order and purpose of the life which was gone.

*   *   *

When she reached the Wilbur kitchen, Emma put down the baskets in a corner and hung up her hat. The door to the parlour was closed but voices came from behind it. Emma dipped water from the bucket into the basin and washed her face and hands; she was about to go up to the attic but stopped at the sight of a valise standing near the foot of the staircase. It was handsome but rather worn, and on top of it lay a thick black shawl neatly folded. Emma stared at the objects and listened to the voices. Mrs. Wilbur spoke seldom; the strange lady talked in a cool and steady voice but Emma could not distinguish any words. At first the voice seemed pleasant but after a moment Emma commented to herself that there was in it something quietly persistent and unstoppable.

She shivered suddenly and turned to run out into the yard. But a vagrant draft slammed the door at the foot of the stairs, startling her and halting her where she stood.

'Emma?'

It was Mrs. Wilbur, calling to her from the parlour. Emma balanced on her toes, still ready to run. Why should Mrs. Wilbur want her? Perhaps to ask her to make tea? They had used up all the real tea, but there was some of Mrs. Bates' herb tea left.

And then, with a jolt, she realized that the visitor might have something to do with her and John. Could the Wilburs have arranged to pass the orphans on to someone else? Could this lady have come to look them over? It was a grim possibility — but surely, Emma thought, as her mind scurried over the past summer, she and her brother had been useful to the Wilburs? And *surely* the Wilburs would have discussed such a plan with them first!

'*Emma*?'

She could still run away, but sooner or later she would have to come back. She paused a moment longer, smoothed her hair and her dress, then bravely and reluctantly opened the parlour door.

'Yes, Mrs. Wilbur?'

'Come on in here, will ya?'

Emma took two steps forward, keeping her eyes on the familiar things: the spinning wheel, the bundles of fleece, the basket of mending. She knew that this was a childish way to behave, but she was not used to strangers and the shattering thought of a moment ago had destroyed what poise she ever had.

28

'There you are, then,' said Mrs. Wilbur. 'This here's Emma, Mrs. . . . . er . . . . Mrs. McPhail. Come on, Emma.'

Emma came a little further into the room.

The lady in the black dress was sitting on the settle, as erectly and firmly as she had sat on the seat of the buckboard. Emma's eyes moved no higher than the large bosom adorned with a vertical row of small black buttons; she was unable to keep from thinking about the stays that held that bosom up. The lady's hands, no longer in gloves, lay in her lap and Emma's attention was caught by their movement: one hand clasped and loosened the other in a rhythmic yet curiously alarming motion.

The girl bobbed a curtsey and looked at Mrs. Wilbur.

'Emma, dear,' said that lady, 'this here's Mrs. McPhail, from York, your aunt.'

Aunt! Emma's eyes flew to the visitor's face. 'But I thought you moved to Boston!' She blurted it out before recalling her manners; as she bent her blushing face she sensed that her words, besides being discourteous, had also been in some way a wrong move.

The cool, imperturbable voice spoke. 'I moved to Boston some years ago, as no doubt your father told you. Now I am living in York again.'

'I didn't know,' Emma mumbled, unable to explain how impossibly remote Boston seemed or how irreversible such a move had looked to her. An aunt in Boston might as well not exist at all.

The only thing Emma had known of her aunt, whom none of her family except her father had actually met, was that she was the younger half-sister of Martin Anderson and that the two of them had been brought up separately. Her mother and father, she recalled, had seemed pleased when she went to Boston. They had maintained no contact with her, nor even mentioned her, after that move. Now, face to face with the aunt, Emma began to understand the lack of contact.

She looked more carefully at the lady's face. She had expected her eyes to be black like the buttons on the dress, but instead they were grey and cool, measuring and assessing Emma. There was the merest touch of grey in the hair which was visible in two symmetrical wings under the edge of the hat, but the face was firm and not old. Emma's look was held for a moment by the eyes as she wondered at their complete absence of feeling, and then she could no longer bear them.

'Well, Emma,' said Mrs. McPhail, 'it's high time we met, don't you think? It is up to us now, and to your little brother, to represent the family.'

'Yes, ma'am.'

'I was explaining to Mrs. Wilbur how I came to hear of your parents' tragic death. Under the will, the three of us are joint heirs.'

'Will?'

'Your father's will.'

Emma looked up in time to see the eyes sharpen slightly, or perhaps only grow colder. 'I didn't know there was a will,' she mumbled.

'Children are usually not aware of such things, and the end came so very quickly. According to its terms, we are all three to have approximately equal shares. Of course I will supervise your portion and John's until you are of age.'

Emma looked at Mrs. Wilbur, who was staring at the visitor in mute awe.

'Of course your late father left nothing besides the farm, which we will probably be able to sell . . . .'

'Sell the farm? But that's home!'

Mrs. McPhail smiled. 'Come now, what use would a farm be to us? We will be living in York, and you and John will grow up in a quite different way from now on.'

'Living in York?'

'Child, stop repeating my words like that!' Mrs. McPhail spoke sharply and Emma flinched as though she had been struck. The lady took a breath and went on in her usual controlled voice. 'I have come to arrange for the sale of the farm and to take you and John back to York with me. Your neighbours here have been very kind, but from now on the family must look after its own.'

A stunned silence followed this decree. Emma glanced again at Mrs. Wilbur but already she knew that there would be no help from that source. Indeed, Emma was not quite sure what help she needed. She knew only that she must resist this pressure somehow. She resented being addressed and treated as a child, and she feared this calmly assertive grey-eyed woman who had suddenly appeared and who had already decided everything. The friendly ease and disorder of the Wilburs was all at once very appealing. Emma remembered her dissatisfaction with them and with her own lack of an imaginable future, but this was not what she had visualized. Her parents would have guided her life; this woman would steer it, channel it, control it.

Then Emma had a moment's remorse. She was making judgments too quickly, no doubt because of the sudden sense of urgency that had come upon her. She looked again at the visitor, trying to be reasonable. For one thing, Mrs. McPhail was clearly not a working-class woman; the hands, temporarily still, were handsome, efficient-looking, and not much worn by hard work. And the face was not unattractive, though its expressionless calm still made Emma uneasy.

'What sort of house do you live in?' Emma asked abruptly, prompted by a yearning to find out more about this stranger, something that might help her to be fair and that might quiet the irrational dread inside her.

Mrs. McPhail smiled condescendingly, making Emma realize that she had phrased the question childishly. 'Oh, quite a large house, Emma, with a verandah and a garden. You may wish to do some of the gardening to remind you of your life on the farm. Will that please you?'

It wouldn't please her, Emma thought vexedly, and it certainly didn't answer her question. What she had really wanted to know was whether there was a Mr. McPhail alive, how he (or his widow, if she was a widow) earned a living, whether there were books in the house. The lady's answer, in fact, concealed far more than it revealed. Emma, who now dared to look steadily at the visitor, thought that the concealment was deliberate. It was a new idea to her that words could be used to hide or mask something rather than illuminate it. At the same time she realized that if she wanted information from this lady, she would have to set about obtaining it in a different way. In particular, she must never again blurt out things in that thoughtless manner. She too would have to be reserved in order to protect herself.

'Well, Emma, have you made up your mind about me?' Mrs. McPhail asked.

Emma paused a moment, then said, 'I must talk to John first.'

'Hmphm! A fine thing when two children think they can decide such matters for themselves.' Then, as though finished with Emma for the time being, she turned to Mrs. Wilbur. 'Is

SHANTY SHELF

there an inn in the village? It will obviously be too far for me to travel back and forth to Waterdown every day. Or perhaps some respectable woman who lets lodgings?'

'There's no village, not what you'd call a village. And we've got no bed to spare now, what with Emma and John extra and the bed that used to be in the kitchen moved upstairs. Can you think of anything, Emma?'

Emma considered that Mr. and Mrs. Wilbur might give up their room and sleep temporarily in one of the attic beds, with some of the children moved to a straw mattress on the attic floor, but such an idea would have to come from Mrs. Wilbur herself. Emma would volunteer nothing towards accommodating Mrs. McPhail. She simply shook her head.

'If I might make a suggestion,' Mrs. McPhail said, observing their perplexity, 'as I arrived I noticed a cabin across the road that seemed to be in good repair . . . .'

'Oh, not our shanty!' Emma exclaimed, forgetting to be reserved and thinking only of that cold March day when she had stood beside the sheeted corpses. Mrs. McPhail couldn't sleep there! It would be outrageous to lodge her under the roof where her parents and small sisters had last lain.

'Is that your late father's farm? I thought it might be. Well, a pallet on the floor of that cabin would serve me for a few nights. The weather is not cold yet.'

'No need to sleep on the floor, ma'am,' said Mrs. Wilbur. 'There's a sort of bed, and a table, ain't there, Emma? Other travellers — workingmen and such — have slept there, but I hadn't hardly thought it fitting for a lady like you.'

'If it will keep out most of the wind and rain, it will serve.'

Emma knew that such adaptability was an admirable quality, but at that moment it made the lady — she couldn't think of her as 'aunt' — even more formidable. Would nothing daunt her? For a second Emma wondered whether to tell her that the shanty had served as a morgue, but she remembered the dangers of blurting out things. This knowledge she would keep to herself.

In any case, the moment for speaking of it was gone. The visitor was on her feet, and Mrs. Wilbur was directing Emma to take linen and blankets to the shanty for making the bed — which was only a straw mattress lying on a low, wide platform built against one wall — and to take a broom and . . . .

'Thank you, Mrs. Wilbur. The child can't carry everything at once. I will go with her and send her back for whatever is necessary.'

Mrs. McPhail carried her own valise and shawl; after her walked Emma with a broom and a bucket which would be filled at the stream where it passed close to the shanty. But it was Emma who unlatched the door of the little building. When she stepped inside, the first thing that caught her eye was the careful pile of bark and kindling which she had laid together on the morning when the bodies were brought in here. It had never been burned. Emma had seen it every time she had come here all during the summer, on those visits which were partly a retreat from the rowdiness of the Wilbur family and partly a vigil of grief. In the instant before Mrs. McPhail entered the shanty, Emma sensed that the small unlit fire had suddenly lost some of its meaning for her. Under the pressure of these new developments, the past slipped behind a veil of distance that slightly dimmed and muffled it.

Emma swept the floor of the shanty. She put fresh straw in the mattress and made the bed and brought firewood and kindling. Mrs. McPhail would eat her meals with the Wilburs but she might need a fire to counteract the morning and evening chill. Emma fetched an old kettle to hang in the fireplace and a basin and chamberpot, a tablecloth and two cups and saucers.

Out of the valise came a Bible, a small packet of tea, a hairbrush and comb, a small mirror, candles, and a maroon-velvet bag containing needlework. Presumably there was also clothing in the valise, but Emma saw nothing of that. Finally the lady produced a tinderbox — saying that she never travelled without one — and, expertly, put flame to the bark and kindling which had lain ready on the hearth for six months.

When Emma left for the last time, the cabin looked as though Mrs. McPhail was firmly lodged in it. Emma wondered where the spirits of her parents and little sisters had gone.

CHAPTER THREE

When Mrs. McPhail came to the Wilburs' house for supper that evening, her hat had been replaced by a small ornamental cap but for the rest she had made no changes. She brought the bag of needlework and, before supper, stitched at her embroidery with the air of one whose hands were seldom allowed to be still — though their present occupation was a much pleasanter one to watch than the clutching motion which Emma had observed earlier. The embroidery was an intricate pattern of flowers along the edge of some soft, white fabric; Emma, busy preparing supper, craned her neck to look more closely at the lovely work until she caught Mrs. McPhail's cool eye and withdrew into herself again.

Mrs. McPhail was settled in the kitchen before Mr. Wilbur and the young people returned from the potato field. When the shouting voices and rattling cart were heard in the yard, Mrs. Wilbur picked up soap and a towel and slipped out. Emma knew she was going to tell her husband about the visitor, and she knew that Mrs. McPhail knew it too. We're acting as though she'd come to spy on us, Emma thought resentfully — and then she wondered which she resented more, Mrs. McPhail's intrusion or Mrs. Wilbur's defensive action. Predictably the harvesters, when they came in, were subdued in manner and cleaner than usual, their hair still wet with creek water and their sleeves decorously rolled down.

As always, supper was a mixed meal of leftovers and some bread. Mrs. McPhail accepted everything — the unplanned muddle of food, the children's bad table manners, the blatantly inquisitive looks of Mrs. Wilbur — with a calmness that dismayed Emma. The tranquility might be a mark of politeness and sophistication, and therefore commendable, but to Emma it was like an impenetrable veneer, inflexible and almost inhuman, behind which somewhere the real Mrs. McPhail lived.

Mrs. McPhail sat next to Mr. Wilbur, on a proper chair for which space had been made by pushing the children's bench further along the table. John sat on her other side, and Emma opposite.

'You are ten years old, I believe, John?' the visitor asked.
'Yes'm. Nearly eleven.' He looked at her steadily for a moment, then went on eating his supper.

When John had been introduced to her along with the Wilbur children he had been just as silent and awkward as they were. Now, as the meal got under way, the Wilbur children were becoming noisy again, even though Mrs. Wilbur was trying distractedly to keep some order at her end of the table. But John, either because of the proximity of Mrs. McPhail or because he remembered something of the Anderson ways, was quiet. Emma had wondered earlier in the summer whether, if he were soon removed from the influence of the Wilbur boys, he could still be taught good manners. She had doubted it then, but now she was a bit more hopeful.

She tried to see him with Mrs. McPhail's eyes: a typical boy, barefoot and poorly dressed, his sandy hair plastered down with water. But as she studied him, Emma realized that he was not shy of Mrs. McPhail. He'd get along with her better than I could, Emma thought; he already has the secretiveness that I must learn.

'What do you enjoy doing, John?' Mrs. McPhail asked. 'What would you like to be when you grow up?'

'I like horses, ma'am. I want to have a farm with nothing but horses — and of course fields for hay and feed,' he added in a tone of adult sagacity.

'That is a very ambitious plan.'

John gave her another look, longer this time and with something speculative in it. Mrs. McPhail looked down at him, and Emma watched them both.

Then Mr. Wilbur spoke. 'Mrs. McPhail, ma'am, just what is your relation to the children?'

She turned gracefully to him. 'I am their father's half-sister. Martin's mother died when Martin was about seven years old; soon after that our father married my mother, and Martin went to live with his uncle, an army chaplain, east of Kingston on the St. Lawrence River. My parents moved to York before I was born; I hardly knew Martin, though I did meet him once or twice when he came to York as a young man to join the army.' She took a sip of water, then went on. 'We maintained very little contact, Martin and I. So you see, we were really strangers. My parents, and Martin's uncle, are dead long since.'

'And now Martin and Anne are dead too, and their two youngest,' said Mr. Wilbur meditatively. 'Sort of an unlucky family.'

Mrs. McPhail looked at him with a smile that barely covered something much less amiable. 'Oh, I'm not so sure of that, Mr. Wilbur. Luck is what you make it.'

'Luck is . . . ?' Emma began impulsively, wanting clarification of such a paradoxical statement. With her parents, there would now be a vigorous discussion of the implication of the words. But she swallowed what she had been going to ask and bent her hot face. She tucked the phrase in her memory, however, to be thought about later. *Luck is what you make it.* Could that really be true?

'Speaking of deaths,' Mrs. McPhail went on, as though Emma had not said anything, 'I believe Martin's uncle, the chaplain, also died in a fire.'

'I don't know nothing about that, ma'am,' said Mr. Wilbur.

'Did your father ever tell you about it, child?' Mrs. McPhail asked Emma.

'Yes, ma'am. It was when his church burned down. He went in to try to save the books and vessels.' This summer she had often thought of those two fires, her mind full of flames and the horror of burning to death. Lately, though, she had begun to understand her father better as a result of the parallel between the two events, and now she found that she had actually spoken quite calmly.

Mr. Wilbur addressed Mrs. McPhail again. 'How did you come to hear about your brother's death, ma'am? It's been six months now.'

Emma, looking at him, realized that he was sizing the visitor up. He had a sharpness that his wife lacked, and Emma saw that he was wary about Mrs. McPhail.

'I was notified by Martin's lawyer in Dundas. I am the executrix of my half-brother's will, as well as being one of the heirs. When the will was made, I was married to my first husband; later he died and I remarried and of course changed my name and address, so that the lawyer had some difficulty in finding me. I lived in Boston for two or three years, though now I am settled in York again.'

So there *was* a Mr. McPhail, Emma thought. If he at all resembled his wife, they would be a formidable pair.

'What is your husband's line of work, ma'am?' asked Mr. Wilbur.

37

'He passed away last year.'

There was an automatic silence, and Emma thought regretfully that after such a statement there could be no more questions. But Mr. Wilbur, after a moment, pressed on.

'What are your plans for Emma and John, ma'am?'

'Why, I shall see to it that they grow up to be well-behaved and useful people,' Mrs. McPhail said, as though no other answer was possible.

An extra degree of wariness came into Jake Wilbur's eyes. He was clearly not satisfied and was considering how to phrase his next question. 'Will you send them to school? Book-learning was pretty important to Martin and Anne, and they'd have wanted the young'uns to get as much of it as they could.'

Mrs. McPhail gave him a bland look but her left hand twitched and then disappeared under the table. 'I quite agree that education is valuable and I am aware that these children, living in such a remote area, have had no chance to attend school. But any child of my brother's must have had a certain amount of teaching at home. When I am better acquainted with Emma and John I will decide what further education is necessary or appropriate.'

Like other statements of Mrs. McPhail's, that one was apparently designed to close the discussion. But Emma could see that the question had not really been answered. She glanced at Mrs. McPhail, who was now calmly eating, and then at Mr. Wilbur, who was frowning absent-mindedly at his empty plate.

'Do you live right in the town of York, ma'am, or outside?' he asked.

'Oh, in the town itself, on a quiet street but not far from the shops.'

So there were some subjects, Emma thought, on which evasion was not necessary.

'I guess it ain't easy for a widow, all alone — though I reckon you must have someone, a companion or . . . . ?'

Emma held her breath waiting for the answer to this vital question. Mrs. McPhail's household — family, companions, servants, or whatever — would have as much impact on the children's daily life in York as the lady herself did. But no answer came. In a ladylike but inexorable way, Mrs. McPhail disregarded the question and turned to Emma.

'Do you enjoy needlework, child?'

38

Emma would have liked to repeat Mr. Wilbur's unanswered question but knew that she would receive no reply. She would wait for a chance to get the information in some other way. Meanwhile, there was wisdom in a certain amount of meekness.

'Yes, sometimes, ma'am, though I've not done anything but plain sewing.'

As she answered, Emma realized that Mrs. McPhail had hardly ever called her anything other than 'child.' It annoyed her. As long as Mrs. McPhail regarded her as a child, the two of them would never be able to make contact. And suddenly Emma knew that the lady was deliberately keeping it so. She's going to hold us down and make all the decisions herself, she thought. She thinks she's inherited us and the farm together in one lump, that we belong completely to her!

Emma was also coming to the conclusion that Mrs. McPhail was pleased about something. It was hard to believe that she could be delighted at being suddenly made responsible for two half-grown children, or at having to spend several days living in a shanty in the backwoods. Still, she seemed to be almost gloating, as though she had made a profit on a business deal. Little of this showed in her outward demeanour except a quiet complacency; Emma sensed it, not in detail but as a whiff of an undefined danger.

Mr. Wilbur spoke again. 'Just what did Martin's will say about the farm, ma'am? I mean about inheriting it.' But his manner was no longer wary or combative; Emma saw that he was yielding to Mrs. McPhail, letting her have her way.

'Well, naturally the will provided for various contingencies. If Martin had been the only one to die, his wife would have inherited everything. Because they died together, I am the children's guardian. The proceeds from selling the farm will be divided into three approximately equal shares. The children will inherit theirs on their twenty-first birthdays.'

So her father had arranged this. But why had he told the children so little about this relative of theirs? And if he disliked her, why had he given her such a prominent part in the will? Probably, thought Emma sadly, because there was no one else.

Emma handed the milk to Mr. Wilbur and glanced at John. He had been listening intermittently to the adults' conversation but gave no sign of realizing its importance. Now he was

DINNER TABLE

having a silent shin-kicking competition with Ted Wilbur, who sat across the table from him.

Supper ended. Mr. Wilbur and the boys still had to unload the potatoes from the cart, and Emma to do the evening milking. Mrs. McPhail, at Mrs. Wilbur's suggestion, moved with her embroidery to the parlour.

In the yard, before going to do their separate chores, Emma and Mr. Wilbur paused for a moment. Mr. Wilbur was frowning again. 'Funny, the way she answered some questions but not others.'

'She's hiding something,' Emma said.

'I guess so. But if your dad's lawyer talked to her, she must be . . . well, she must be all right. Maybe she's just shy.'

'Shy!'

'Well, you know. Not wanting to talk about herself.'

'Maybe,' Emma murmured doubtfully, again torn between being fair to strangers and being cautious about them. The one thing that came to her clearly as she did the milking, though, was that Mr. Wilbur had done his best for her and could do nothing more to counteract Mrs. McPhail's power. From now on Emma was on her own.

* * *

After finishing the milking, Emma wondered whether she too was expected to go to the parlour. But before anyone could say anything, she went through Mr. and Mrs. Wilbur's bedroom to Granny's room. She took with her a basket of grapes to be stripped off the stems and a bucket for the loose fruit.

Once inside Granny's room, she felt safe for the first time since Mrs. McPhail's arrival. She stood against the door for a moment, then put down the basket and bucket and drew a deep breath.

'Well, Emma.'

'Hello, Granny.'

Granny was a long, thin shape in the bed. In spite of the warm day and the closed window, she had a blanket over her. It was dark outside now, except for some moonlight, and Emma could barely see her.

'Light us a candle, my dear,' said the old voice from the pillow.

'Yes, Granny.' Emma took the candle to the kitchen and lit it

BEDSIDE

at the fire on the hearth, then went back to the quiet front bedroom.

'Now, then, Emma, tell me what's wrong.'

Emma smiled a little. 'Why should anything be wrong?' She moved aside the tray of supper dishes which had been still lying across Granny's legs. Emma was surprised to find herself speaking so lightly, but she did feel better for being in this room, as though the indefinable menace of Mrs. McPhail had shrunk somewhat.

Only now that she was here, in this quiet backwater of the noisy and disorganized house, did Emma realize how uneasy she had been. During the meal her attention had been so concentrated on Mrs. McPhail and on her interactions with John and with Mr. Wilbur that she hardly knew what food she had eaten. She was still frightened and didn't know why. As she stood beside the bed staring over it at the wall, she realized that she was rigid with tension. She wriggled her shoulders fretfully, then sat down where the blanket padded the upright wooden edge of the bed-frame.

'Well, girl, what's the matter? This afternoon I heard someone in there' — Granny pointed at the closed connecting door to the parlour — 'talking to Liza but couldn't hear none of the words. Then when Mary brought me my supper, she said as how your aunt's come. I didn't know you had an aunt.'

'She says she's our aunt.' Emma spoke softly, aware of the proximity of Mrs. McPhail in the parlour — Mrs. McPhail, whose ears might be sharper than Granny's and hear more through the thin partitions.

'Says! You mean you don't believe her?'

'Oh, I suppose I do. Father had a half-sister, I know that, though he never talked about her, and it was Father's lawyer who found her, so I suppose she's real.' Emma looked down at the hands clenched in her lap. For the first time since the various shocks of the afternoon and evening, she was trying to sort out how she felt. The grapes, brought along from a sense of duty, stood forgotten near the door.

'Well, so then she's your aunt. What's she like?'

'Scary.' Emma looked at the old woman, searching for some kind of support, but the hollow eyes were shadowed by the candlelight.

'How do you mean, scary?'

'I don't know. Strong. And smart. She's going to take us away to York. She lives in York.'

'Well, that'll be a change for you. Don't you want to go?' Granny's words might be encouraging, but her tone was neutral.

'I think I would like to see York, but not in this way. Not with some stranger. If it had been with Mother and Father . . . .' She lifted her clenched hands to her mouth in a tense gesture but then lowered them again. Abruptly she leaned towards Granny and whispered. 'She doesn't tell us anything about herself, how she lives or anything. She's a widow . . .'

'Poor?'

'No, I don't think so. Not rich, but not poor either. And she treats me like a child.'

The old woman gave a sardonic little smile but said nothing. Emma flushed and suddenly spread her hands in a gesture of appeal. 'I know I'm not grown up yet, Granny, but she treats me . . . .' The outstretched hands fisted for a moment. 'She's trying to ignore me, to make me into something like . . . like a dog. Something that can't answer back, only obey. Something that she can ignore, that she can just not consider. I *hate* that, Granny. No one's ever done that to me before. I don't know what to do about it.'

'That's probably what scares you most, Emma.'

'Yes. It scares me half to death. Can she . . . do we have to do exactly what she says?'

'If she's your guardian . . . .'

'She says she is. She says Father decided it in his will. Do we have to do just what she says?'

'I don't know, girl. A lawyer would know.'

They stared at each other, not having to put into words the fact that there was no lawyer nearby to consult.

After a moment, Granny spoke again. 'Where's your father's lawyer? In York?'

'No, in Dundas.'

'Oh, yes, I remember he used to go there the odd time.'

'You know Dundas well, don't you?'

'Oh, yes, I know it. We lived there for a few years, George and me, till we came up here.' Granny often talked about this. 'We used to visit there sometimes even after we came to live here. We'd go for shopping and suchlike. It made a bit of a treat for George and me. You can get things there that the ped-

44

dler don't carry. I used to have stomach trouble and got a powder from a nice apothecary called Mr. Mackenzie. He's an important man in York now, writes newspapers and sits in the government, by what I hear.'

'Mr. William Lyon Mackenzie who writes the *Colonial Advocate* newspaper?'

'I guess that's the fellow. How did you know?'

'Father had a few of the papers. He said Mr. Mackenzie would do great things one day.'

'Well, I reckon that could be true.' She gave a dry old chuckle. 'Bigger things'n mixing up powders for an old woman's stomach, I can tell you.'

They were silent for a moment. Emma moved to the chair and began stripping the grapes off their stems, dropping the fruit with a soft patter into the bucket at her feet and gathering the empty stems into her apron. But her mind was working on a different subject. As far as she could see, the first thing they needed was some advice from a lawyer. She wanted to know what the will, and the law, committed her to. The will, so suddenly an influence in her life, was like the voice of her father come from the dead, giving instructions. She would obey her aunt if it was really her father's wish that she should do so, but she needed to be sure. The lawyer seemed, so far as she could see, to be the source of truth in this matter; moreover, he had presumably met and talked with both her father and Mrs. McPhail, which made him all at once come close.

But how was she to reach the lawyer? Would they let her go to Dundas?

Then she caught the glimpse of an idea.

'Have you got any of that powder left, Granny? The powder for your stomach?'

'Goodness, no, girl, it was used up long ago.'

'Don't you need some more?'

The old woman and the girl looked at each other steadily, and Emma's hands dropped into the apron idle among the grape stems.

'I could get . . . .' Emma began, at the same time as Granny said, 'You could go . . . .'

They laughed and Granny took precedence, speaking even more softly than she had been doing. 'You could go to Dundas to get me some more of the powder. And see the lawyer. Do you know his name? Would your aunt tell you his name?'

GRAPES

Emma shook her head, thinking of Mrs. McPhail. 'No, I don't think she would.' Then she brightened. 'Would she tell you, Granny? If you were to . . . not ask, maybe, but just . . . .'

'I'll see what I can do. You must bring her in to meet me, as soon as you can. Do you think you could go to Dundas by yourself?'

'I think so. Asking my way, of course.' Emma hesitated for a moment. 'I'd . . . I'd have to dress nice to talk to a lawyer. And I haven't got any good clothes.'

'Leave it to me to think about that. I've got nothing else to do all day but think.' She chuckled again; it was a rumble that started deep inside her and bounced along inside her body — Emma visualized it bumping upwards against each separate piece of Granny's backbone. 'That powder, now — I really do need it. Lying down, my stomach don't get the exercise it needs.'

She looked at Emma, and Emma looked back. There was an agreement between them. Granny poked a long finger towards the parlour. 'And I'll find out from that woman what the lawyer's name is. You may have to leave us alone for a bit.'

Emma nodded. 'How far is it to Dundas?'

'I couldn't say what it is in miles. If the weather's good, it'll take you three or four hours walking there, maybe more. And longer back 'cause that's uphill. Along with what you have to do when you get there, you'd best spend the night.'

This was a new idea to Emma; she frowned down at the grapes, which her fingers were automatically stripping. 'Where? I mean, where'll I sleep?'

'Leave me think that over too.' Out loud she made a mental note. 'Clothes for Emma, and where'll she sleep.'

'And the lawyer's name from Mrs. McPhail.'

'Yes, yes, that's the first thing. Though you understand, when we talk to the others we only tell them about the powder.'

'Naturally.'

Some of Emma's gloom had faded now that she had spoken of her misgivings to someone else and now that she had the prospect of actually doing something. She hoped that Mr. and Mrs. Wilbur would allow her to go to Dundas — the powder for Granny's stomach seemed such a very inadequate reason. But Granny could be a nuisance when she wanted something, and she had ways of making sure that she got the powder and that it was Emma who went to buy it. Two days away from home, though, and such a distance! The strangeness was daunting, and for a moment a wave of fear roared over her. But it had to be done, and no one else would do it if she did not.

Emma continued stripping grapes, talking with Granny about one thing or another. During the summer, ever since that horrible morning after the fire, the two of them had grown close together. Granny had been a good friend to the Andersons; now that the old lady was bedridden, Emma could repay that friendship. Besides, the two of them, invalid and orphan, seemed to have peculiar places on the fringe of the Wilbur family.

As a result, Emma spent nearly every evening in this room, sewing or mending or doing jobs such as this one. Sometimes she read aloud from the Bible, the one book that Granny owned. Neither of them could make sense of many parts of it, but they liked the words and the stories. Often some passage would start Granny reminiscing. Emma had heard many times how she and her husband George, dead ten years now, left the rebellious colonies to the south during the Revolutionary War, 'not because we were Loyalists, not really — George wasn't loyal to nothing besides himself — but because he always had to be moving. We'd have been gone from here by now if he was alive still.'

All the adults Emma knew or had ever heard of had moved house several times in their lives. Until now she had never moved and, indeed, had never travelled further than Waterdown. At the end of this evening, as she gathered up the clutter of grapes and stems, bucket and basket, she realized that going to York with Mrs. McPhail would mean leaving Granny — not only leaving the old lady to the comparative neglect of her family but also leaving behind her own sole friend and advisor. She said nothing of it, not wanting to make Granny unhappy, but she noted it as another reason for resisting the York plan if — or for as long as — she could.

CHAPTER FOUR

On the following morning, Granny Wilbur asked Emma to help her into her clean nightgown and cap; then her room had to be put into especially tidy order, and finally Emma brought Mrs. McPhail — who had been sitting in the parlour with her embroidery — to meet Granny.

'Thank you, Emma, you may leave us,' said the old lady, and Emma went back to the kitchen to resume work on the grapes, smiling to herself at Granny's sudden dignity. But she understood it well enough. Granny had her ways of compensating for being generally neglected, and a little pretense of being the family matriarch instead of a burdensome old invalid was only natural. Perhaps, too, Mrs. McPhail might be impressed to find that Emma was not friendless. Whatever the reason, Emma admired Granny for putting on the external signs of her innate dignity and was grateful for the effort.

But then, thinking of Mrs. McPhail's impenetrable manner, she wondered whether Granny's efforts would have any effect. Rebelliously, stripping grapes off their stems with more force than necessary and with spurts of juice going to waste on apron and floor, Emma hoped that she would never be expected to embrace her aunt; she shuddered at the thought of touching that solid-looking bolster of a bosom, with its row of black buttons.

But after a few minutes, her irritation simmered down a bit, as it often did when she thought of the less frightening aspects of Mrs. McPhail. The embroidery was really lovely, for instance; and early that morning, when Emma had looked out of the attic window, she had seen Mrs. McPhail walking briskly along the road, evidently taking a constitutional. She moved with vigour and energy; indeed, in spite of her ample bosom she was not a heavy woman. Her waist was slim and her age, as estimated by Mrs. Wilbur that morning before breakfast, was about thirty-five. 'I'll bet you anything she ain't never had a baby,' Mrs. Wilbur had said, stirring the porridge.

'Why? How can you tell?' Emma had asked.

'That waist. Can't keep a waist like that after having a baby.'

'I think she wears stays.'

'Stays can't make a fat lady thin.'

As for Mrs. McPhail's age, Emma thought Mrs. Wilbur might well be right. Martin Anderson would have been forty-three on his next birthday; his half-sister might well be no more than thirty-five. Emma remembered the sight of that briskly walking figure, and then across that image came the chill of the grey eyes that gave nothing away. She was confused and frightened again, and hoped that something would come of the talk with Granny.

It was not until the evening, after she had set the grapes to ferment in a crock in the dairy corner, that Emma could find time to go to Granny's room. She took a lighted candle with her and sat down.

'Here's the name of the lawyer, Emma. See, I've written it down for you. Mr. Jameson. I didn't get the name of the street where he lives, but you can ask around for him. You could go first to the pharmacy store and see if they can give you directions to Mr. Jameson's house.'

Emma nodded. 'Yes, Granny. Thank you. But you'd better keep the paper here until I'm ready to go to Dundas. I've no place to keep it. And you'll have to write down the name of the powder for me.'

'Yes, yes, I wasn't forgetting. Although I'm not sure that I remember the name just right. I'll put down what I remember, and then you can tell the man that it's for an old woman who's lying down all the time and her stomach don't get the exercise it should.' The bumping chuckle came again.

'What did you think of Mrs. McPhail?' Emma asked.

'D'you know, Emma, if it wasn't for the fact that she wanted to take you away, I think I could almost like her.'

'*Like* her!' Emma's world shook to its foundations.

'I don't mean I could be fond of her, but I could admire her. She's some woman.'

'How do you mean?'

'She knows what she wants and sets out to get it, though I don't know but what she might break a law here or there to do it. She's had some education — you can tell by the way she talks. She's done pretty well for herself.'

'I think she's dangerous.'

'Yes, she might be that.'

'Then how can you admire her, Granny? Dangerous people are . . . well, are dangerous.'

50

Granny laughed. 'O'course they are. Dangerous don't mean, though, that she's all wicked — though there's probably some wickedness in her. Good people can be dangerous too.'

'Can they?' asked Emma, frowning.

'Sure. They can be dangerous to bad people, for instance.'

'Well, of course, but . . . .' It was becoming too tangled. 'She's so . . . strong, and she makes me feel helpless. It's awful to be young, Granny, and in the power of someone like that.'

'Yes, of course. But old people're also in the power of others, don't forget.'

The look of grieved resignation on the wrinkled face made Emma realize again how difficult Granny's life would be if she, Emma, were no longer here. Of course this only complicated things, but at this moment Emma thought more of the old lady than of her own predicament.

Then Granny turned her face aside slightly. Emma knew the sign well. 'You're tired out, Granny.'

'Yes, girl, I am. Bring me a glass of water and then I'll say goodnight.' They both knew that Granny would hardly sleep during the night but that her spirit needed to withdraw into whatever silent space it sought when it needed repose.

Emma brought a glass of water, plumped the pillows, helped with the chamber pot, and then gave Granny a warm hug. She saw a glint of tears in the old woman's eyes, and went out without a further word, brooding on such an ending to such a life and amazed that, in spite of a lifetime of hardship and a long illness, there was still so *much* of Granny.

She had only just closed the door of Granny's room and was standing in the other bedroom, half brooding and half listening to Mrs. McPhail's voice coming from the parlour, when Mary came running up to her.

'What's the matter?' Emma asked, feeling as though in the past two days she had grown to be much more than five years older than Mary.

'It's Isaac Bates. He's at the back door.'

'Well, I suppose he wants your dad.'

'No, he wants you.' Mary giggled. 'He has that look.'

'What look?'

'I don't know. The look men get. Go on, Emma.' And she gave her a teasing little push.

Through the kitchen window, Emma saw Isaac Bates sitting

BAKING

on a sawhorse in the back shed. The evening was cool after the warmth of the day, and Emma picked up a shawl before going out to him.

'Hello, Isaac.'

'Lo, Emma,' he said, standing up.

'Mary said you wanted to see me.'

'Come away from the house a bit.'

Emma hesitated and looked at him carefully; a gleam of light from the kitchen window caught his face and showed it to be very earnest, but the eyes remained in dark shadow. Again she saw an unfamiliar side of Isaac and drew back a trifle.

'No, no . . . .' she began, and then said more steadily, 'Let's just sit here by the light from the kitchen.'

'Sure, if that'll make you easier.'

But, though she felt more comfortable close to the faint light, he apparently didn't. He fidgeted in his pockets and then began to puff hard at his pipe as if it were going out, although Emma could see quite clearly that it wasn't. Because he seemed to have come with some purpose, Emma did not feel it right to begin an unimportant subject of conversation. She sat beside him on the sawhorse, waiting for him to speak.

Eventually he did turn to her, gazing at her with that direct, rather questioning look before averting his eyes again.

'I bin thinking,' he said. 'This lady visitor . . . I hear she's planning to take you away to the city.'

'My aunt,' Emma said, surprised to find herself feeling the tiniest bit of pride in the connection.

'Yeah. Your aunt. You goin' with her?'

'I don't know yet. I . . . .' She was about to tell about the planned visit to the lawyer but remembered in time not to. 'I just don't know.'

'I bin thinking,' he began again. 'You know I got a farm of my own now. Well, it ain't a farm yet but it will be. 'Bout six miles up-country.'

'Yes, I heard about it.'

'You're young yet, Emma,' he suddenly said in a rush, 'but in maybe a year you'll be thinking of marrying. If you was to take me, marry me, you could stay here. I mean stay in the country, come and live on my farm.'

'Marry you?' she asked, hedging a bit because he had surprised her and because she needed time to think.

'Not right away but, like I said, in a year maybe. If the Wilburs can't keep you, my mother'll be glad to have you live with her. I'll be building a shanty on my farm come spring and then in summer, or the fall, we could get married and live there.' He lifted his eyes to hers for a moment, then stared off into the dark again.

'John . . . .'

'John too,' Isaac said hastily. 'Glad to have him. He can help a lot and be company for you.'

'Oh, Isaac,' she said fretfully, putting her hands to the sides of her head, 'I can't tell *what* to do.'

'No need to tell me tonight. Think about it. But once you've gone to the city it won't be so easy to come back.'

She saw the truth of that and wondered at Isaac seeing it too. She warmed towards him, and remembered that her father had always said that Isaac was wasted in the backwoods.

No, it wouldn't be so easy to come back, once she had been to the city. She could picture the bush farm, slowly being cleared with such immense labour. Would she want to come back when she was old enough to marry Isaac?

She shook her head firmly, not in answer to Isaac or herself but as an admonishment to think no more about it now.

'Thank you for your offer, Isaac. It's thoughtful of you.' But even she, inexperienced as she was, knew that in connection with such an offer as this he should have said something about loving her, wanting her for his wife, wanting to spend the rest of his life with her. Perhaps he ought to kiss her, though his acknowledgement of her youth suggested that that might not come until later.

And then suddenly she had to choke down a laugh. Here she was, just having received a proposal of marriage, sitting beside an apparently glum suitor on a sawhorse, with everything kept as businesslike as could be imagined. Surely the arranged marriages about which she had read and heard could not have been less romantic than this! She was annoyed for a moment, wondering how on earth Isaac expected her to accept such a lukewarm offer, and then she was uneasy, wondering whether his whole plan had been devised out of nothing more than a sort of awkward kindness and pity.

She stood up; all this would take a good deal of sorting out, and she saw no benefit in talking to Isaac any longer now.

'I've got to think about it, Isaac.'

'Yeah, sure, that's what I expected.' He got up too and then, before she could turn away, he took her hands in both of his. She still could not see his eyes, but the gesture touched her deeply. His hands were hard with work, but warm and dry and strong. They enfolded hers with a protectiveness she had not known since her father's death. And she realized that perhaps only delicacy was keeping him from kissing her or talking about love.

She blushed, ashamed of having belittled him in her thoughts and glad to see him in a different way now. In spite of the blush, which she hoped he couldn't see, she looked up into his face again, wanting something a little further, some more insight into this surprising inner Isaac, but he only said softly, 'G'night, then, Emma,' and turned away into the darkness of the yard.

CHAPTER FIVE

The next evening, Granny Wilbur put on even more of her dignity. After supper she asked her son to carry her to the kitchen, where she had herself installed in the chair by the fireplace. Occasions such as these were rare and made a great impression on the Wilburs who, since Granny's attack, had very quickly come to exclude and ignore the old lady. But once she was sitting in the big chair, wearing her best shawl and cap, and with a blanket around her legs, she had a presence and influence like those of a monarch enthroned. It was as though she had risen from the dead, an impression enhanced by her gaunt face and skeletal hands. Emma was used to the old lady and, on these evenings, derived a quiet amusement from watching the reactions of the rest of the family.

Her purpose in joining them tonight was the matter of Emma's trip to Dundas to fetch the medicine.

'You ain't used that powder for years,' said Liza Wilbur to her mother-in-law, not in protest but in mild observation.

'What sort of medicine is this?' Mrs. McPhail asked.

'It's for my stomach,' said Granny Wilbur. 'What with lying down so much, my stomach don't get the exercise it needs.'

'Is there nothing else you can take, such as prunes? There must be something which is easier to come by than a powder which can be bought only in Dundas.'

Granny's face went stubborn, but her eyes were watchful. 'An old woman like me's got a right to have the things she's used to, to make her comfortable. And prunes got to come from the store too, in Waterdown or in Dundas.'

'Why must it be Emma who goes?' Mrs. McPhail's obstinacy was not as visible as Granny's but everyone in the kitchen sensed it. Bess, picking burrs out of the dog's coat, looked up at Mrs. McPhail with a vacant, wondering expression much like her mother's. Mary's darning needle stabbed air while her eyes too were on the visitor. Jake Wilbur's fingers moved more slowly over the new axe-handle that he was shaping. The three boys stopped their subdued punching and kicking of each other.

Granny spoke. 'There's no one else to send. She'll only be

gone two days. But Jake and the boys are all busy with the harvesting, and now that Aggie's married, Emma's the only one old enough to go. Liza can do without her help for a couple of days. And now's the time, 'fore it rains and the roads get bad.'

The two women faced each other across the fireplace, in which a small fire burned. Emma, sitting on the bench beside the kitchen table, stopped sewing to watch them. It was a contest of personalities, Granny claiming the privilege of age and Mrs. McPhail the advantage of being Emma's aunt and guardian. Emma understood something of what was in Granny's mind, but Mrs. McPhail's was impenetrable.

'Very well,' Mrs. McPhail said at last. 'Emma may go to Dundas. I wish, though, that I knew of a respectable house where she could spend the night.'

'I will see about that,' said Granny magisterially. 'I have friends in Dundas.'

'When she comes back,' said Liza Wilbur, bent over her mending, 'I suppose she'll have to be thinking about going with you to the city, ma'am. When was you thinking of going back? That's unless she decides to take Isaac Bates.'

Mrs. McPhail ignored the last remark. 'I will be here for a week or so still, Mrs. Wilbur, and when I leave I shall take Emma and John with me.'

'So you're staying on, ma'am?' Jake asked.

She turned to him. 'I am expecting any day a visit from a gentleman who may be interested in buying the Anderson farm.'

All eyes turned on her once more, and again the air was tense.

'A York man would that be?' asked Jake Wilbur. 'Is he planning to move here and work the farm?'

'No, I don't believe he wants to operate it as a farm. But it would be a good investment for him.'

'There's too many people buying farms for investment,' Mr. Wilbur commented, apparently calmly but with an angry undertone. 'What with the Clergy lands and the property being bought and held idle by the rich, the land ain't but half settled and them that lives on it has to carry twice the load of building roads and bridges. And how'll we ever get villages and churches and schools that way?'

Mrs. McPhail smiled as if to suggest superior insight into the workings of the government and the economy, but she said nothing.

'Will you really sell the farm?' Emma asked. She had a frightening vision of not being able any longer to stand beside the ruined house, of facing a strange gate shutting her out from her home.

'See whether this York man'll let us pick the grapes in the fall,' said Liza Wilbur. 'It'd be a shame to have all them grapes just dropping off and going to waste. And the rhubarb in poor Mrs. Anderson's garden.'

Mrs. McPhail laughed, but the mood in the kitchen remained heavy. 'I don't even know yet whether he will buy it. Do not let us create problems where none exist.' She turned off the smile that the laughter had left on her face. 'Of course if anyone in this neighbourhood made an offer to buy the Anderson farm, I would consider the matter.'

Jake Wilbur grunted. 'Not likely. Who's got the money to buy a made farm? Anyone who needs more land or a place for himself takes up empty land. Cheaper, except in sweat, and we've all got lots of that.'

Granny gave her son a stern glance, but he was peering with one eye along the axe-handle and did not notice the silent reprimand. The old lady turned to Mrs. McPhail. 'Is the gentleman who's coming from York a friend of yours, ma'am?'

'A friend, yes, and in some sense a business associate.'

'Are you in business yourself, ma'am?' Granny asked. Emma held her breath and waited for the answer.

Mrs. McPhail produced a chilly smile. 'There are not many businesses in which a lady can engage, Mrs. Wilbur. Though I must say that in a rapidly growing city like York, there is room for enterprise and hard work.'

Emma stitched mechanically, still hoping that Mrs. McPhail could be lured or provoked into giving some information.

Granny went on. 'What kind of . . . ?' when Liza interrupted. 'Lord, I do think you're smart, Mrs. McPhail, ma'am, being in business and talking to lawyers and all. I'd be scared silly.'

Emma looked up. Liza was stooped over the mending basket on the floor at her feet; Mrs. McPhail was looking at her bent head with cold eyes and a thin smile; Granny, foiled in her search for information by her daughter-in-law's foolishness, looked at Emma with a face infinitely old but with a faintly sardonic gleam in her eyes.

* * *

59

Two days later, Emma set off for Dundas. She had been up early to help with the milking and the poultry and the family breakfast. Then she had changed into the better of her two handed-down dresses and a pair of Granny's boots. The boots were somewhat too large and had bits of rag stuffed into the toes, but they seemed comfortable enough and were better looking than Mrs. Bates' old ones that Emma had been wearing all summer since outgrowing the ones she had saved from the fire. Granny also lent her a shabby black cloak. Emma had no proper hat or bonnet, but to the cloak was attached a hood which could be pulled up when needed. In a cloth bundle she carried some apples and boiled potatoes to see her through the two days. Tucked safely into the pocket of her dress was the tinderbox, which she regarded as a sort of talisman, and the all-important slip of paper describing Granny's stomach powder and giving the name of the lawyer who had prepared Martin Anderson's will. Also written on the paper were the names of three ladies whom Granny had known when she lived near Dundas.

'But that was years and years ago,' Emma had said. 'Will they still be there?'

'Maybe not all, but one of them's bound to be. They're all respectable people. You can ask for directions when you get to Dundas.'

'But . . . can I just go up and knock and . . . . ?' Emma was used to backwoods hospitality; in the absence of inns, travellers could and did ask for lodging at the nearest house, and the Anderson shanty had sometimes sheltered strangers as it now housed Mrs. McPhail, but she had not thought that the same thing could be done in towns.

'Yes, you can. Say I sent you. Martha Wilbur.' The old lady chuckled. 'Don't say Granny Wilbur — they wouldn't know who you meant.'

'Martha Wilbur,' Emma repeated obediently.

'They're all good women, and none of them would think of letting you go to a hotel by yourself. Of course they might not have a bed, and you might have to sleep on the floor . . . .'

'Oh, that's all right.'

'And here,' Granny said, reaching out and dropping two English penny pieces into Emma's hand. 'That's all Jake could spare. One's for the powder — that ought to be enough unless the pharmacist man has turned crook and swindler. And *that* ain't impossible neither, come to think of it.'

'What's the other penny for?'

'It's for the lady you spend the night with. Likely she won't take it, but if she's real poor or if you think she'll take it, offer it to her.' Granny frowned in deep meditation. 'O'course, some people might consider it an insult to be offered money for doing a person a kindness.'

'How can I tell?'

'I don't know, girl, you'll have to work it out for yourself. See whether you're treated more as a friend of mine or as just anyone who's given a lodging out of charity. Then, if it's charity, you can pay your money and not feel so bad. A penny ain't much but it's just for a night's sleeping space; if you get given breakfast you can always help with the washing up or something.'

Emma had nodded, though it sounded complicated. She would think it over later and get it clear in her mind.

The weather, on the morning of her departure, was hazy and a bit cooler than on the former days. Goldenrod and Michaelmas daisies flourished by the roadside, squirrels were busy among the trees, and the air was full of dancing insects.

The road, after passing alongside the cleared and partly cleared fields of the Wilbur farm, crossed the creek. There was a narrow footbridge for pedestrians and a ford for everything else. Beyond the creek was the forest, and here the road was a mere track marked by ruts and by blazes chipped with an axe in the bark of trees. It wound through the forest, avoiding large trees, stumps, fallen logs, and boulders. Mr. Wilbur or one of the Bates men, when travelling to Waterdown and in not too much of a hurry, sometimes stopped on the way to cut off an overhanging branch, but otherwise it was not a made road. In places, on this dry day, it was dusty; elsewhere it was grown with grass and weeds, or soft with fallen pine needles; almost everywhere it was criss-crossed by exposed roots.

Emma had travelled to Waterdown several times before, when her parents were alive, so that this part of her journey was familiar. She walked along in good heart, cheerfully circumventing logs and sometimes, in spite of her age and responsibilities, skipping for a few steps. The trip to Dundas would (she did not let herself doubt it) lead to her gaining useful information from the lawyer. Furthermore, it was a two-days' release from the problems and chores of her ordinary life.

61

PUMPKIN FIELD

As Emma walked, enjoying the strange sensation of being alone and away from her accustomed world, she watched a bevy of sparrows having a dust bath and admired the flash and shriek of a pair of bluejays disappearing among the trees. Out of sight, and in different directions, two woodpeckers were busy sounding like confused echoes of each other. A chipmunk, acorn in mouth, sat motionless on a log while she passed.

But gradually she stopped noticing the scenery and thought about the big problems of which she seemed to be the centre. She could neither like nor trust Mrs. McPhail and, though asked to do so, had not brought herself to call her Aunt Harriet. Yet she had come to understand why Granny Wilbur could admire her in some way. The visitor had brought a whiff of a larger world into the farmhouse; she sometimes talked about life in York — a concert she had attended, a new style in hats, a college for boys which had opened recently — though still without saying anything informative about her own circumstances. The way she spoke reminded Emma a little of her parents. She realized that Mrs. McPhail was worth emulating in that respect. At the same time, she observed that the visitor could persuade any of the Wilburs, except possibly Granny, to agree to anything. They would be of no use in resisting Mrs. McPhail if Emma needed help in any such endeavour. The woman had power, though Emma had not yet found out where the power came from, and it was that that made her frightening.

The proposal from Isaac Bates had given Emma much to think about. Isaac had been part of her life ever since she could remember; he was one of the Bates boys who had, for a small wage, helped her father with the clearing of the Andersons' first fields. She liked Isaac without ever having thought about it. During these last few days she had seen him in a new light, but the thought of marrying him and moving to the bush was not appealing. She knew the back-breaking, mind-stifling work required to clear land; she knew how primitive those first shanties were, how close to bare survival they'd be living. It would be starting all over again from the beginning, just when her own life had reached some level of civilization. And Isaac's new farm was six miles away, so that she would not even be able to have much contact with the Wilburs.

And yet, was it not a safer prospect than going to York with

Mrs. McPhail? It was impossible for Emma to picture her life there. The visitor's secretiveness had given rise to strange conjectures; last night in bed, Mary had reported the Bateses' opinion that Mrs. McPhail was very rich and that the Anderson children would be brought up in luxury — and also, conversely, that she was involved in the white-slave trade and had horrible plans for her young relations. Emma didn't believe either possibility but did find it strange that the woman avoided saying anything about how she lived in York. She had said that there was a school to which John could go — though she understood that he could already read and write and cipher, and as for further education . . . she only shrugged and shook her head. There was apparently no way of discovering what she really had in mind for Emma and John.

She and Emma had briefly discussed Isaac's offer. 'Of course, if you intend to marry this young man,' Mrs. McPhail had said, 'you will pass from my care into his. I suppose I would give my consent — there would be little point in withholding it.' But her manner conveyed that she did not for a moment think that Emma would choose to marry Isaac.

While thinking, Emma had been steadily walking along, and soon she came to the swampy stretch which, after rainy weather, was impassable to vehicles. Mr. Wilbur and the Bates men had talked about cutting trees and laying them down to make a corduroy road in the worst places, but nothing had come of it yet. Today, however, the swamp was muddy only in a few places and Emma navigated it by balancing on logs and taking advantage of every bit of dry ground padded with cedar needles.

Eventually she reached Bakersville, which consisted of a few houses and a sawmill on the Grindstone Creek that went on to flow through Waterdown. Emma crossed the creek near the mill. In the yard stood two oxen hitched to a huge log being delivered for sawing, and a wagon loaded with cut lumber. The millwheel turned with much creaking, and she could hear men's voices and then the sudden shriek of the saw.

From there to Waterdown, about two miles away, the land was mostly cleared. The fields were divided from each other and from the road by rough fences. Harvesting and fall ploughing were going on. The sight of such advanced civilization made the prospect of living on a bushfarm less attractive than ever. She walked on, half happy and half brooding, towards Waterdown.

CHAPTER SIX

Waterdown, on this late-September day, was little more than a few buildings at a dusty crossroads. The main road from York to Dundas went through it from east to west; the gristmill where the Andersons used to have their wheat ground was just to the south of this road, on the Grindstone Creek. Emma did not go near the mill; she had to follow the westerly road to reach Dundas. But she idled past the general store, wishing that she had a reason to go in. She had been there with her parents, and now she gloated over such remembered treasures as raisins, bolts of cloth, kitchen equipment, boots, and ribbons.

When she left the store behind and resumed her way to Dundas, her feet faltered a little. This was, for the first time, unfamiliar ground. But she couldn't slow down. It must be past mid-day and she had miles to go still, and errands to do before nightfall. Now that she was actually on strange territory, the prospects of finding her way to the pharmacy, and talking to the lawyer, and asking one of Granny's friends for a night's lodging, scared her. She ought to stop and eat something out of her bundle but nervousness took away her appetite and she walked on.

The road soon changed its character. It began to go downhill in irregular bursts. This must be the beginning of the valley in which, Granny had said, Dundas was located. But there were too many trees all around for Emma to see ahead.

Just then, she heard the creak and rattle of a cart behind her. Two other carts had passed her in the course of the morning, and several horsemen, and one or two pedestrians. Most of the people had greeted her but all had gone on their way. This cart, however, stopped.

'Give you a ride, little lady?'

She turned nervously. She had been afraid of this, knowing that it was sometimes unsafe to accept offered rides but being aware by now of the tiredness in her legs and feet.

At first she took the person on the cart to be a man. But when she looked again she saw that it was an elderly woman, wrinkled and sunburned, in a man's cap and coat but wearing

INN

a skirt hitched up to reveal woollen stockings and sturdy boots.

'Yes, please, ma'am,' said Emma, using the spokes of the big wheel to climb to the seat.

The woman flipped the reins on the horse's back and they started down another sharp little hill. The horse moved slowly and carefully over the rough road. Emma clutched the side of the cart for support against the jolting. There was no chance to talk, but Emma was glad to rest her feet.

After one particularly heavy jolt, Emma heard something falling off the back of the cart.

'Oh, look!' she cried, drawing the woman's attention to it.

'Hunh!' grunted the woman. She stopped the horse, dismounted, and walked back. During the halt, Emma looked around. Below her and to the left, visible through a gap in the trees, there was a steep drop with a glint of water at the bottom.

'What's that? A river?' she asked.

The woman, having loaded the sack onto the cart again, climbed to her seat. 'Cootes' Paradise,' she said.

Emma was puzzled. 'I beg your pardon?'

'Cootes' Paradise. Swampy land where the English soldiers used to shoot ducks and geese. One of the fellers was called Cootes. He had a funny notion of paradise, that one. Like I say, it's just a swamp full of birds and other critturs. My husband used to hunt there sometimes, and other folk. I live nearby to it and can hear the shooting. There's a creek flows through it down to the lake, and ships go up the creek to get from the lake to Dundas.' She clucked to the horse and the jolting resumed.

When they reached a stretch of road that sloped more gently and was not so very rough, the woman asked, 'Goin' to Dundas, are you?'

'Yes'm.'

Granny had warned Emma not to talk about her errand — 'You never know who you're talking to. And a closed mouth passes for wise with most folks.'

'Come a long way?'

'Yes, quite long. Do you live near here?'

'Bottom of the hill. I run my own farm since my husband died. I been visiting my daughter who's married up the hill a piece.'

'Do you work a farm all by yourself?' Emma asked in wonderment.

'I got a man comes in who'does the real heavy work.' She chuckled in a way that made Emma think of witches in fairy tales. Emma studied the woman covertly: the sinewy hands on the reins, the dark eyes among the wrinkles, the grey hair knotted into a small tight bun. There was something about her which recalled Mrs. McPhail — perhaps the sense that they were both independent women. Emma was a little afraid, but she felt somehow enriched by the contact with the funny old woman in the man's cap.

The cart turned in at a driveway and stopped. 'Here's where you'll have to get off, little lady.'

'Is this your farm?'

'Yup.' The woman gave her wicked chuckle again. 'Come and visit me when you're in these parts again.'

It seemed meant as a joke, if one could judge by the old woman's grin, and though Emma could not see the point of it she smiled, resolving not to accept the invitation. She scrambled down but at the last moment kept one hand on the side of the cart. 'How far is it to town? . . . to Dundas, I mean?'

'Just a short walk now, girl. Keep on along this road and you can't miss it.'

Emma spoke her thanks and went on. The road continued downhill, rolling and curving; to her left, when she had a view among trees or over cleared fields, she caught glimpses of the creek and could tell by that how much the road was descending. At one of the gaps she stopped and stared; a ship with a sail was moving over the water. She watched till it was out of sight and then walked on again with a lighter heart; the ship, unlike the strange old woman, was a new experience with no tinge of danger about it.

Abruptly she reached the bottom of the valley. At this point, the land was almost all cleared and there were frequent clusters of farm buildings, then the even closer ranks of a town. She walked along, staring everywhere about her, until she was alarmed by trampling hooves and a loud bellow. 'Hi, there, watch where y're goin'! Wanna get kilt or somethin'?'

She fled out of the road to the doorway of the nearest building, in time to avoid being run down by a six-horse team drawing a huge wagon loaded with barrels. The shirt-sleeved driver glowered at her as he passed. From then on she stayed close to the side of the road, out of the way of the thickening traffic of riders on horseback, carriages, small wagons, and a couple of men pushing wheelbarrows.

But she had little time for idling and staring about. She wanted to do her errands in what was left of the afternoon so that she could start for home as soon as possible the next morning.

She asked two housewives with baskets to direct her to Mr. Mackenzie's pharmacy.

'Mackenzie's?' one of them asked, looking puzzled.

'That's Lesslie's now,' said the other. 'Mr. Mackenzie is gone but Mr. Lesslie keeps the store.'

'Where is it, please, ma'am?'

'Why, back along here, just this side of the corner. You must have walked right past it.'

Emma returned the way she had come. In a moment she found herself in front of the pharmacy and went in.

The door tinkled; she looked about her in alarm at the sound but when the tinkle came again as she closed the door, she thought it must be all right. A young man behind a counter smiled at her and she went to him timidly to explain about Granny Wilbur and her powder. Before she got very far in her story, he interrupted.

'You'll have to talk to Mr. Lesslie, miss.'

'Aren't you Mr. Lesslie?'

He laughed. 'Oh, no, I'm just a clerk.'

Emma wasn't quite sure what a clerk was, but this person looked very splendid to her with his clean hands and smooth hair and clothes that were finer than anything her father had worn even for best.

'May I speak to Mr. Lesslie, then, please?'

'He's just stepped out, but he'll be back in a few minutes. Why don't you look around the store until he comes back?'

The store was a wonderland. Emma had imagined that a pharmacy sold only medicines, but here there were candies and tobacco and ink and bandages — and then she saw the books, several shelves of them against part of the back wall. In a dream she walked towards them, awed by the dark rows.

She turned to the young man who, having nothing else to do, was watching her. 'Do you sell them? Or are they learned books about medicines?'

He laughed. 'No, it's Mr. Mackenzie's circulating library.'

APOTHECARY'S SCALES

'But Mr. Mackenzie is no longer here.'

'No, he left these behind. He believed in people having books to read. So does Mr. Lesslie.'

'You mean a person can read them? Take them away?'

'Yes, people can borrow them for a certain period of time, and then return them so that others can have a turn.'

'May I touch them, even if I'm not borrowing? I live far away and . . . .'

'Sure, go ahead. Sit down and read, if you like, till Mr. Lesslie comes.'

She turned back to the books. But she couldn't choose any one book that she especially wanted to read. Without touching, she read the titles on the spines. There were books about travel and history and famous people, books she had heard her father mention, such as *The Decline and Fall of the Roman Empire* and Boswell's *Life of Johnson*. There were her old friends Addison and Steele, and Shakespeare, and Sir Walter Scott . . . .

'You were looking for me, miss?' came a voice from behind her.

She whirled around, shaken out of her dream.

'Oh! Oh, yes! I came about Granny Wilbur's powder.'

The man smiled. 'Who is Granny Wilbur, and what is her powder supposed to do?'

Emma dug in her pocket. 'It's written down on a paper. She's an old lady who has to lie down all the time. The powder is for her stomach, to make it work right. She used to get this powder from Mr. Mackenzie . . . .' She held out the slip of paper, pointing to the line of shaky writing that concerned the powder. 'You are Mr. Lesslie, aren't you?'

'Oh, yes.' He took the paper and read what was written there. 'It'll take a few minutes to make up.'

'May I wait here . . . with the books?'

'Certainly, miss. I won't be very long.'

She turned back to the books. If there'd been only one book, she would have had the courage to take it down and read. But the shelves full of them dazzled and daunted her.

In spite of what he had said, Mr. Lesslie seemed to be taking a very long time making up the medicine. Emma began to tire of the ranks of books and then they grew misty and unsteady before her eyes. Suddenly she found herself leaning against the shelves and then sliding to the floor. The door tinkled once or twice, and then after a blurry moment she felt a hand on her forehead.

'Passed out,' a voice said.

'Get her some water. And she's probably half-starved. Find me those biscuits in the back room.' That was Mr. Lesslie's voice, she thought.

When she opened her eyes, she was sitting on a low stool with her back against the wall. The young man was offering her a glass of water and a large homemade cookie, both of which she took gratefully. 'You had a long trip today?' he asked.

'I walked for hours,' she said, too tired to varnish the plain fact.

'You'd best be finding a place to spend the night.'

'Is it night already?' she cried, jumping off the stool. 'But I have to see Mr. Jameson still.'

'The lawyer?'

'Yes, do you know where he lives?'

'Sure. Just turn right when you walk out this door and then left at the next main intersection and to the second cross-street after that. His office is in his house — you'll see the brass plate by the door.'

When Mr. Lesslie handed her the packet of powder, she put one of the penny pieces on the counter. She looked up; his eyes were unexpressive and he seemed suddenly the man of business, quite unlike the man who a few minutes earlier had seen to it that she was given a glass of water and a cookie. And, now that she thought about it, perhaps she ought to pay for the cookie as well. Quickly she laid the second penny beside the first.

'Is it . . . is it enough? It's all I have. And Granny does need . . . .' She looked up appealingly. She was nearly as tall as he was but felt at a great disadvantage.

'Then it'll have to be enough, won't it?'

She thought he was trying to be jovial but she couldn't make out what he really thought; she was only chilled by his words.

He put the money in a drawer. The nice young man was gone; Emma would have liked to thank him and say good-bye. She put the packet of powder carefully in her pocket, next to the slip of paper and the tinderbox.

'Can your Granny read?' Mr. Lesslie asked as Emma opened

the tinkling door. 'I've written directions on the outside — how she's to take the medicine. But if she can't read I'll tell you and then you can . . . .'

'Oh, no, Granny can read,' Emma said quickly. She was about to explain that the old lady was not actually her own grandmother, but she realized that that was of no concern to the pharmacist. Emma had never before been so aware of the insignificance of herself and everything that mattered to her. She left the store, tired and bewildered and wishing that she were at home. The day was darkening and she had better hurry.

As she went up the street, it occurred to her that she had forgotten to ask Mr. Lesslie for help in finding Mrs. McDonnell or one of the other ladies on Granny's list. But she could ask Mr. Jameson.

To her relief, she found his house with no difficulty. There was the brass plate with his name on it, and up four steps was the door. The front of the house was high and austere, with the windows arranged in a regular pattern. She thought of an engraving in one of her father's books, and remembered her father saying that a house could — and if possible should — be more than just a shelter.

She drew the hood up over her head, then went up the steps and pulled the bell-handle. As she waited, she realized that some of the urgency — today's urgency, at least, though not the deep and long-range anxiety — had fallen from her. This house was the destination of today's long journey; she had reached it at last; its owner was her source of information and perhaps help.

Really, she thought, she was handling the strangeness of town remarkably well! — except for fainting, but that could not be helped. She had not lost her way nor her belongings; she had completed one errand and was about to perform the second.

And, in the glow of this satisfaction, she remembered with pleasure the books. How delightful it would be to live within reach of books! Moving to York — where there would certainly also be books — was suddenly a more pleasing prospect. She thought she could put up with almost anything from Mrs. McPhail if there were a library nearby.

Abruptly the door opened; she had almost forgotten where

THE LAWYER'S HALL

she was. A well-dressed maid stood in the doorway. 'Yes?'

'I've come to see Mr. Jameson,' Emma said carefully, drawing herself up tall.

'He's busy, miss.'

'I can wait. I've come a long distance especially to see him. My father, who is dead, knew him.'

'Is it business?'

This daunted Emma for a moment. 'Yes, I guess so. It's about law matters.'

The maid looked scornful. 'Wait here, I'll see. Name, please?'

'Miss Emma Anderson, from Flamborough Township, near Waterdown.'

The maid pushed the door until it was nearly closed, then clicked something to hold it in place. Emma waited on the step in the deepening dusk. She would have liked to eat something before this interview; now Mr. Lesslie's biscuit would have to see her through.

In a few moments the door opened again. 'Come in and wait in the hall,' the maid said. 'You can sit there.'

Emma sat down on a high-backed bench against one wall. The hallway was dim and chilly but handsome, with doors of dark wood in each wall. A staircase rose out of it and curved near the top, where it disappeared out of sight. By way of furniture there was a dresser and a table as well as a coat-rack and the bench, but it was obviously not a room for living in, just for walking through. On a bracket was a clock whose tick filled the hall; Emma would have liked to look at it from close by but dared not walk across to it because the maid was hovering at the back of the hall.

A man-servant came to light a couple of candles that stood on the table; he whispered something to the maid as he passed, and she giggled.

After some time, one of the doors opened; voices came out, and then two gentlemen. Emma was awed by their upright figures, their handsome clothes. They walked past without paying attention to Emma; then the taller and grander one showed the other out. When the front door was shut again he turned to Emma.

'Yes? You are the girl from Flamborough Township?'

She stood up. 'Yes, sir. Emma Anderson. Are you Mr. Jameson?'

'Indeed I am, unless I've been sailing under false colours for a very long time.' He laughed at his own joke. 'Come in, come in.'

The room seemed beautiful to her. The light of several candles reflected off the glossy bindings of books, the dull shine of leather-upholstered furniture, and the glass-fronted maps and pictures on the walls. There was a fire on the hearth; Emma hadn't realized until then how cold she had become while sitting in the hall, and she was glad of the warmth.

Mr. Jameson took his place behind a big writing table. 'Sit down, Emma.'

She sat on the edge of a chair and clutched her hands tightly together. She had not imagined this splendour, which seemed to take away her self-satisfaction and the words she had been planning to say.

'Emma Anderson,' said the lawyer musingly. 'You'll be the daughter of Martin Anderson, who died some months ago? An aunt of yours came to me recently to make enquiries about the will and about your place of residence.'

'Yes, sir. She's staying with us now — with the Wilburs, I mean, who took in my brother and me after the fire.'

'And what did you wish to see me about? Your aunt is your guardian now, is she not?'

'Yes, sir. So she says. I wanted to ask . . . one thing I wanted to know is, do we have to do what she tells us?'

'How do you mean?'

'She wants to take us to York.' Emma swallowed.

'Don't you want to go to York?'

'It's not that so much. But she's our guardian now and . . . and do we, John and I, have to do what she says?'

'What would you rather do?' he asked. 'Do you want to stay with your friends in Flamborough?'

The clear statement of alternatives made Emma feel dreadfully lost and alone. That, and the tension and exhaustion of the day, brought tears to the very brim of her eyes. She sniffed and groped for her handkerchief.

'There, there,' the lawyer said in a detached but kindly voice. 'Tell me what is really worrying you.'

She looked up at him. 'I don't like my aunt very much.'

'You don't? I thought she seemed a very capable and sensible woman.'

'I think she's dangerous.'

The lawyer was silent for a moment. He was used to people from the back townships who came to him inarticulate, angry, worried, and of course unable to pay his fees. So far the girl had been like them, except that she spoke a little better. He had attributed this to parents somewhat more educated than their present station in life suggested; it was a common enough situation.

But suddenly out of the muddle of the girl's talk had come this observation: 'I think she's dangerous.' The girl might well be right, because he remembered the aunt — unquestioningly sure of herself, gracious rather than pleasant, and a great deal more businesslike than he thought becoming in a lady. Yes, the girl might be right in this one sharp observation. And yet it would be folly to encourage her in her fears. If she was perceptive and clever, the girl had better stand or fall with the hard-headed aunt rather than certainly fall — or at least sink, wither, and coarsen — on a farm in the back townships.

He looked at the girl again, seeing her as a human being instead of a client; he noted the thin face, the russet hair springing out from around the edges of the black hood, the large eyes.

'How old are you, Emma?' he asked.

'Just fourteen, sir. John is not yet eleven. I have to look after him till he's a bit older.'

'But your aunt is going to look after both of you now. I think you're lucky to be in the care of such a capable lady.' He was testing her to see how she would respond.

'Did she say to you . . . did she tell you what she intended to do with us?'

'I thought you just informed me that she intended to take you to York.'

'Yes, but I mean . . . I mean, sir, that I can't see what it will be *like* in York, in what sort of house we'll live, whether John will go to school. Is Mrs. McPhail rich? She's trying to sell our farm, although I'd rather . . . .'

The lawyer placed the tips of his fingers carefully together. The girl was a disappointment after all. 'It would be easier to help you if you knew just precisely what you wanted to ask me. You are not expressing yourself very clearly. And it is growing late.'

She blew her nose again and sat straighter. 'First of all, then, sir, do my brother and I have to do whatever my aunt says?'

'As long as she is your legal guardian, yes. You may appeal to her good nature to try to change her plans, and if she should order you to do something unlawful . . . .' He shrugged. 'Of course if you marry, she ceases to be your guardian. Is that clear so far?'

'Then she *is* allowed to sell the farm,' Emma said.

He gave a deep sigh. 'I'll tell you about the will, Emma. You've a right to know what it says.' He went to a cupboard, opened it, and took down one of several boxes ranged on the shelves inside. After sorting through the contents, he brought a single sheet of paper back to the writing table with him. Emma watched every movement and trembled when she saw what must be the will that her father had actually touched and signed.

The lawyer scanned it, then put it down and looked at Emma. 'I'll explain it as simply as I can. In the event that both your father and mother died, and left some children young enough to need a guardian, your aunt was to be that guardian. Your father knew that there would not be much to inherit but he also knew that your aunt would have to be recompensed — paid something — for looking after the child or children. So he decided that the farm should be sold, including the livestock or whatever, and that Mrs. McPhail would receive one-quarter of the proceeds of the sale. The rest would be put in a trust for the surviving children, who would each receive an equal share of that on his or her twenty-first birthday. When the money is in a trust, your aunt can't touch it.'

Emma was frowning. '*She* said our three shares — hers and John's and mine — would be equal. Does that come to the same thing as . . . as what you just said?'

'Are you sure she said the three shares would be equal?'

'Approximately equal, I think she said.'

Mr. Jameson pursed his lips and pondered. 'Do you know anything about fractions, Emma?'

'You mean in arithmetic? No, sir. I was just starting multiplication when . . . .'

'Yes, quite so. Well, look here.' He rose and went to the fireplace; on the mantelpiece he found a long wooden splinter of the sort used to lift a bit of flame from the hearth to a cigar or a candle. When he was sitting behind the writing table again he leaned forward and so did Emma. 'One-quarter of this bit of wood is about so much.' He broke off a piece. 'That's what your aunt will receive. You and your brother will each get half of what's left.' He broke the larger part of the splinter in two and laid the pieces on the desk alongside the shorter one, aligning them all with a finicky finger.

Emma looked at them. 'That's not equal shares. Not even approximately.'

'No.' But Mr. Jameson saw no reason to believe that the aunt had been deliberately lying. There would seem to be little point in such a lie, and she might only have been simplifying matters for the backwoods folk. As he recalled Mrs. McPhail's calculating eyes, he did just wonder. But it would do no good to feed this girl's uneasiness and suspicion.

'So the farm has to be sold to produce some money,' Emma stated.

'Yes, because your aunt must have her share immediately. She will have expenses.'

Emma sat thinking, and the lawyer watched her. There was something in the girl after all.

'The clothes and things she buys for us . . . will they be paid for out of our share or hers?'

That was a clever question, he admitted to himself. 'The will says nothing about that. But usually such expenses come out of the guardian's share. I did point out to your father that he might be laying rather a heavy load on your aunt's shoulders. And now that the house and contents are lost, and there are two of you to care for, she has a great responsibility.'

Emma frowned again, then looked straight at the lawyer. 'My father did not like my aunt.'

Mr. Jameson's face revealed nothing. 'He trusted her enough to put you in her care. He trusted her to do the best for you, to look after you and your inheritance until you could undertake both of these things yourself.' A log in the fire collapsed and both of them glanced at it; it had the effect of reminding them of the passing of time. 'Was there anything else you wanted to ask me?'

'Yes, I wanted . . . I wondered . . . . Do you know anything about Mrs. McPhail's life in York?'

'Why, no, nothing really, except that she's a widow. She seemed to be an intelligent and efficient lady.' Recalling the aunt once again, and her simplifying of the terms of the will, he had a moment's uneasiness. But what could he do? It was not up to him to question whether Mrs. McPhail was a suitable guardian for the children, and if it became a public issue, the lady would win every point. He had met her kind before.

He nodded firmly at Emma. 'I have no doubt that she is your aunt, and I am sure that she will look after you properly — for the sake of her own good name, at the very least. But Emma, have you asked her what she plans for your future?'

'She never answers . . . not really, not with something specific.'

'Well, if I were you I would go back to her and ask her clearly and precisely. You're a big girl and should be able to find that out. And why not think of this plan of hers as a good thing for you and your brother? Wouldn't you rather be in the city, with all those opportunities for learning and experience, than on a farm in the back townships? If you are a brave and enterprising young woman you can make much of this opening.' He stood up. 'And now I must ask you to leave. Good-bye, Emma.'

He rang a small hand-bell which stood on the desk, and the maid came and showed Emma out.

Only after the door was closed firmly behind her did Emma realize that once again she had forgotten to ask directions to the house of Mrs. McDonnell.

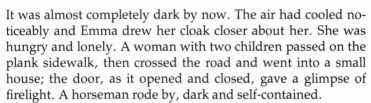

CHAPTER SEVEN

It was almost completely dark by now. The air had cooled noticeably and Emma drew her cloak closer about her. She was hungry and lonely. A woman with two children passed on the plank sidewalk, then crossed the road and went into a small house; the door, as it opened and closed, gave a glimpse of firelight. A horseman rode by, dark and self-contained.

But she could not stand all night on Mr. Jameson's stoop, and the approach of drunken shouting from the direction away from town gave her the impetus to move. She went back towards the centre of Dundas; perhaps the pharmacy would still be open and the friendly assistant would direct her to Mrs. McDonnell's house.

The town had totally changed its appearance and character. By daylight it had been full of vehicles and people going about their business, crowded with drays and barrows, housewives and messengers and shirt-sleeved workmen. Now it was much emptier, and dim and secretive. Emma as she walked saw a series of tableaux, some inside the houses revealed by lampglow or firelight, others on the street in the small patches of brightness spreading from open doors or uncurtained windows. In one house a man was beating a dog and she heard the creature howling. Alongside the street two drunks were sitting on a stump, either singing or lamenting or both. A couple of young women walked slowly past Emma; a male passer-by gave them a bold glance, then looked intently at Emma herself.

She hurried on, passing a hotel on the verandah of which half a dozen men sat, their cigar tips glowing in the dark. There was some muttering among them and then a laugh. She reached the place where she expected to see the pharmacy, but she found instead an open-fronted blacksmith shop. The smith was still at work and Emma paused for a moment to watch him and to warm her spirit at the light of the fire. But the ruddy glare could not really dispel the chill of her loneliness.

Besides being lonely, she was also tired and hungry. The hunger at least she could cure, and she began looking for a place where she might rest and eat something of the contents of her bundle.

Eventually she sat down on the stoop in front of a house. There were people inside; she could hear voices and see firelight between the curtains. She began eating a cold boiled potato; she longed for hot soup and a cup of milk but had no money and would in any case have been afraid to venture into a place where these things could be bought. In fact, the whole town frightened her now. The thought of living in York, which had been pleasant when dominated by libraries and friendly shop assistants, was now terrifying. She was too tired and bewildered to reason it all out, but she shrank from everything about her.

She had finished the potato and was eating an apple when the door behind her burst open. She looked up, then started to her feet in alarm. A very large man stood there, swinging a lantern as though it were a weapon.

'Get offa there!' he said angrily. 'Get offa my steps! Tramp! Beat it!'

She fled down the street, clutching her bundle, until she tripped over something. For a moment she lay still, too scared to move, but then she realized that she was not being followed. There was no sign of a lantern and no sound of footsteps, only a dog barking somewhere and some distant laughter. She got up and dusted off her clothes. She had lost the partially eaten apple but had another couple of potatoes left in the bundle; those she would save for breakfast.

Mrs. McDonnell. She should ask for Mrs. McDonnell. Granny Wilbur had described her as a large, warm-hearted woman with several small children — 'though they'd be grown-up now, of course.' If Mrs. McDonnell failed her, there were also a Mrs. Albert Smith and a Mrs. Hutchinson.

Emma looked about her. Clearly she was now walking away from town; there were only a few lights ahead of her. Close by, there was a heavy snuffling sound, probably of a cow or a horse in a pasture.

But going back into town meant going back the way she had come, past the stoop from which she had been chased by the man with the lantern. And now she had nothing at all to pay for her night's lodging. It would be simply begging for favours. Emma realized the helplessness of being without money in strange surroundings.

And then it came to her that she need not, after all, beg for the use of someone's bed or floor. She could sleep outdoors. It was a dry night and not really very cold; she could find a spot somewhere, away from the road, and curl up there. It was dark but she could make out the main features of her surroundings. She walked on, looking about for a likely place.

Soon the road began to climb; remembering the hill she had descended earlier in the day on her way into Dundas, she hoped this meant that she was on the way home, but so far she had seen nothing familiar. Then she came to a barn built close to the road. It might give her shelter for the night. She passed through the open gate and approached the barn warily, wanting to avoid dogs, people, and the inevitable manure pile. There was, however, no smell of fresh manure at this side of the building. The doors were closed but she found, more by touch than sight, a place where some boards leaned aslant against the outside of the barn, at the side away from the house. Under the boards, grass and weeds grew tall and, flattened, would make a pallet for her. She crawled in, curled up in her cloak with the hood bunched up to make a pillow, and slept instantly.

* * *

She woke up gradually and reluctantly, awakened as much by a revival of her sense of urgency as by the thinning of the darkness. She lay a moment without moving, looking at the grass blades close to her eyes and at the comforting protection of the rough boards above her. She was cold through and through, however, and her entire body, as she found out when she began to move, was painful and stiff. Her feet hurt the most; when she crawled out from under the sloping planks and tried to stand up, she had to lean against the barn wall for support and stifle a cry. Her feet and legs would hardly hold her up, and yet she had to walk home today! All those miles!

But first she had to get off this unknown farmer's property. She found a roughly trimmed pole about four feet long and, using that for support, hobbled out through the gate and along the road a few yards to a grassy hummock where she could sit. Behind her a rooster crowed.

She sat down and rubbed her legs. She longed to take off her boots — Granny Wilbur's boots — but her ankles were

83

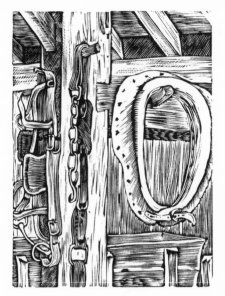

THE HARNESS BEAM

swollen and she was afraid that her feet would be too; if so, she might not be able to put the boots on again.

Then she remembered the stuffing in the toes. She took off the boots, removed the wadded cloth, and put them on again, lacing them much more loosely and not all the way to the top. It was not a comfortable arrangement, but it would have to suffice. And yet, all those miles! She would never be able to walk that far.

She drooped, propping her elbows on her knees and watching a small parade of ants at her feet. One carried a part of a leaf, much bigger than itself. That too looked impossible. She herself had faced impossibilities before. After the fire, it had seemed as though she could not go on living without the sustenance of family life, the life created by her parents and rich with what they themselves had done and thought and read. But she had lived on, finding in herself some bits of that collective existence and making out of them a kind of shanty for the spirit, small and inadequate but still a comfort. Difficulties, then — impossibilities, even — could be overcome. She knew the immense effort it would take, but it could be done.

In any case, she would have to reach the Wilburs' farm tonight, one way or another.

She ate the remaining potatoes in her bundle and folded the handkerchief in which they had been wrapped. Then she was thirsty, and the sound of cows lowing in the barn behind her suggested milk. Emma turned and peered over the snake fence, thickly overgrown with weeds. A door somewhere creaked on its hinges. Hopefully, Emma crept back to the barn. As she approached, she heard a milkmaid talking to the cows.

The milkmaid was already at work when Emma found her. The cow being milked jerked its head and the girl looked up.

'Who're you?'

'A traveller,' Emma said, instinctively quoting from a bedtime story that her mother used to tell.

'What d'you want?' The girl still had her hands on the cow's udder but was looking suspiciously up at Emma.

'A drink of milk, please. I've drunk nothing since yesterday.'

'Get away, you're naught but a beggar. I'll tell the master . . . .' The milkmaid moved the bucket and started to get to her feet.

'Please,' said Emma, putting out a placating hand. 'I work in the dairy too, at the Wilburs'. I'd give you a drink of milk if you came by and needed it. Just out of the edge of the bucket.'

The girl looked furtively about, then got up and handed Emma the wooden bucket, which held about a cupful of milk. Emma took it in both hands, tilted it carefully, and drank all of the milk, warm and frothy as it was. There were four cows waiting to be milked, and a cupful wouldn't be missed.

She handed the bucket back and wiped her mouth. 'Thank you, miss,' she said, wondering how she could really show her gratitude.

'There's leaves in your hair,' said the girl. 'You bin sleeping out? I seen right off that you was a beggar.' She was more curious than angry now.

'No, really I'm not. But I'm a stranger here in Dundas, and I didn't have a place to sleep.' She wasn't going to tell the whole complicated story about Mrs. McDonnell and Mrs. Albert Smith.

It occurred to Emma to ask directions back to Flamborough but just then there came the sound of whistling.

'That's him,' said the milkmaid in a sudden flurry of fright. 'Be off now and don't let him see you. You can hide somewheres.' She dropped to the milking stool again and went on with her work.

The barn was dim, but it was enough like other barns so that Emma could guess her way about. She shrunk into a shadow, watched the man go past and through a doorway, and heard the sound of clanking harness. Like a ghost she ran through the door and down the drive to the road.

Once there, she didn't know which way to turn, right or left. She looked about but everything was strange and there was no sign of Dundas town to be seen. The sky was overcast so there was no sun to give the direction. She began walking up the slope, remembering that she had come downhill into Dundas the day before.

CHAPTER EIGHT

Around the first curve, she saw someone walking towards her. Emma's first impulse was to hide her face in the hood, but then she realized with a shock of surprise that she knew the man. He was the peddler who, two or three times each summer, came up to Flamborough with his cart. He drove no cart today, which was perhaps why she had not recognized him at first, but he carried an empty canvas sack over his shoulder.

He recognized her too. 'Hello! Aren't you a long way from home? What're you doing here?'

She saw him for the first time as a person, not merely as a peddler of necessary and tempting merchandise. He was quite young, with a plain but cheerful face marked by very bushy eyebrows.

'I've been in Dundas doing errands. I'm on my way home now.'

'Oh no, you're not.'

She was puzzled, then frightened. Was he planning to . . . ? She had no words for what she feared, but fairy stories were full of abductions, and even without the cart he looked as though . . . . And hadn't she heard something unpleasant about peddlers? She looked about for help but there was none in sight.

He laughed. 'You're on your way to Ancaster.'

'Ancaster?' She had never heard the name before.

'You're going the wrong way. You're on the wrong side of Dundas. Dundas is there . . .' he pointed down the hill, 'and where you live is beyond Dundas, up that far hill.'

Emma stared down the slope and at the opposite hillside, imagining the time it would take her to walk so far. And even when she reached that distant ridge she'd not nearly be home. She stood in the dusty road in silent wretchedness.

'Cheer up,' the peddler said. 'It's still morning, and in the morning everything is possible. Come along, I'm bound for Dundas myself.'

She turned and walked with him, trying not to break into tears of despair and tiredness and bewilderment.

The peddler gave her a few minutes to master herself. When

THE QUAY

she had blown her nose, he asked her name. 'I've seen you, of course, but I see lots of folks, hundreds of 'em. All I know is that you're from up that way.' He gestured again at the distant blue ridge of land.

'Emma Anderson.'

'The folk who . . . whose house burned down?' He knew the whole story, of course, having heard about the tragedy and having himself spread the news further, from back doors to inn bars to chance encounters on the road. 'Sorry about your Mom and Dad, Emma. Where're you living now?'

'With the Wilburs.'

'I guess I saw you there about June, didn't I?'

'Yes. I bought a straw hat off you, and Mrs. Wilbur bought some buttons and some cotton cloth to make underthings for me.' She remembered the talk about the extravagance of new underwear for Emma when she could perfectly well wear Aggie's cast-offs. But when Emma came out of the first dreadful grief after the fire, she rebelled against wearing other people's underclothes any longer; she hated the other hand-me-downs almost as much but could not afford to reject them. She would, she said, make the new things herself and promised Mrs. Wilbur that if ever she could she'd repay the cost of the cotton material required.

'You'll have had a sad summer,' said the peddler now.

'Yes. Everyone else seems to have forgotten. And now there's a woman — lady, I mean — who says she's our aunt, John's and mine, and who wants to take us to York.' She told the rest of the story, glad of the peddler's sympathetic ear.

By that time they were in the town again. 'Did you say you were going home now?' the peddler asked. 'Or have you got other errands to do?'

'No, I'm going home. Which is the road?'

He gave directions, but still she lingered. 'Which way are you going? Are you on your rounds?' As she said it, she looked doubtfully at the empty sack.

'At this time of the year I only make short trips. Don't want to get stuck in the back townships in the real bad weather. I'm on my way to the quay to pick up some supplies.'

'To . . . to where?'

'The dock . . . you know, where the warehouses are. On the creek.' he laughed. 'You really are a stranger in Dundas, ain't you?'

She blushed but realized that his teasing was friendly — and, in any case, he was right about her being a stranger.

'I didn't know there was a dock in Dundas, though I did know about the ships. Are there ships there now?'

'Can't say. Like to come and see? It ain't much out of your road.'

He resumed his long stride, which she could only just match with much violence to her aching legs. Emma knew that, before he had advanced to the dignity of a cart, he had made his rounds with a pack on his back and even now, to reach an isolated farm, he would leave his cart where the road ended and walk the rest of the way.

The quay was simply a place where the banks of the creek had been raised and reinforced with logs and stones. There were a few small warehouses alongside the open space, and to Emma's delight there were three ships moored at the quay. 'Oh!' she exclaimed, stopping short at the sight. 'Real ships!'

The peddler laughed again. 'Well, maybe. We call them batteaux — that's the little ones — and Durham boats. That end one's a Durham boat. But look, you'd better nip along home. I got business here, and you got a long way to walk today. And them clouds are getting thicker. Hope it don't rain later.'

She was reluctant to leave his company, but of course he was right. She said good-bye and followed his directions to the York Road, the same one down which she had come yesterday. A little way up the hillside she thought she recognized the farm of the funny old woman who had given her a ride.

Beyond that the farms were scattered more thinly. She looked down into the valley but no ship spread its sail on the creek now. After one near-stumble she began watching her footing more carefully; even though it was still morning, she was tired and she did not dare to think about the pain in her feet.

A horseman passed, going up the hill, and two Indian men with packs came downhill. A wagon rattled up behind her; she moved out of the way to let it pass. But when it was beside her it stopped.

'Give you a ride, lady?'

This time it was a man. Emma looked up; he was a burly fellow with hairy arms and a bold eye. She hesitated, not quite liking the look of him but thinking what a help it would be to get a ride even for a mile or two.

'Yes, please,' she said finally.

'Why, I thought you was an old woman,' the man said, and gave a great laugh. 'You was walking like an old woman, all slow and bent over.'

'My feet hurt.'

'Well, come on up, then.'

She climbed in and they set off. The pair of horses moved slowly but even so the wagon jolted and rocked alarmingly, heaving over exposed rocks and roots and through bone-breaking holes.

'You move closer this way,' the man said. 'Don't want you getting tipped out if we hit a big bump.'

But Emma stayed as far away from him as she could, clutching at the side of the wagon with both hands. She didn't at all like him, with his big laugh and his bold eyes. He was perhaps the same age as Isaac Bates, and the arms revealed by his rolled-up shirt sleeves looked immensely strong. She was afraid of him, but her feet hurt very much and she was so tired and battered by all the unusual experiences of these two days that she was glad of the ride. The thrill of seeing the ships had faded in face of the relentless unwinding road that had to be travelled.

'You goin' far, lass?' he asked when he stopped the horses for a breather at the top of a particularly sharp incline.

'To . . .' she began, but then remembered. 'Yes, quite a way. How far are you going?'

'I turn off up here a piece. You goin' on to Waterdown?'

'In that direction,' she said, hoping that she sounded dignified and also wishing to stop his questions. 'It looks as though it might rain.'

The clouds had indeed been darkening gradually and now lay low like a cover across the tops of the high trees along both sides of the road. It was not more than half-light in the narrow tunnel where they were, and there was no house nor another living creature in sight. Again Emma looked apprehensively at the man, but he gave his loud laugh and with a flap of the reins started the horses moving again.

Not much further on he stopped. The forest continued along the right-hand side, crowding in on the twisting road, but on the left was a large field, cleared except for stumps, in which pumpkins grew. A rough track led through the field and beyond, into more woods.

'This here's my road,' the man said, stopping the horses. 'I guess you go straight on. Let me give you a hand off.'

She protested that she could climb off by herself, but he had already dismounted from the wagon and come around to her side, reaching up to help her. The outstretched arms looked strong and sustaining, but in his face she saw something for which she had no name but which she instinctively feared. She pulled back, sliding along the seat, but he grasped her by the waist and lifted her off, then set her on her feet and laughed.

'Funny my thinking you was an old woman, back there,' he said.

'Let me go, please. And thank you for the ride.'

'Oh, no, not yet. Come along, I'll show you something.' He moved his grip to one of her arms. Several raindrops fell onto the hairy back of his hand; Emma had a moment's clear vision of them, caught up on the reddish hair and suspended as they would have been on a spider's web.

He saw the drops too and was distracted for a moment, looking up at the sky in frowning speculation. Both of them knew what rain did to roads.

Then he laughed again. Emma shuddered. 'Come on, girl, this won't take but a minute. You know what I mean, eh?'

His hand gripped her arm above the elbow; he pushed her forward past the horses' heads, and had turned towards the woods when a great clatter came towards them from around a sharp curve in the road. It was two horsemen galloping side by side.

'Jesus God, look out for the wagon!' one of them shouted.

The riders pulled up in a confusion of hoofs, dust, and oaths. A horse whinnied. The hairy hand dropped from Emma's arm and she ran, leaving behind the furious shouting and the tangle of horses and harness. She ran around the curve in the road and kept running until her breath was gone and she had to lean gasping against a tree. The running was agony to her feet but she did not dare sit down to rest them. Before she had properly caught her breath, she again noticed the beginnings of the rain. There was nothing about her that would be damaged by the wet — except Granny's powder, wrapped only in a piece of paper. She reached into her pocket to touch it where it lay next to the tinderbox. But of course! Inside the tinderbox the medicine would be dry.

She took the things out of her pocket and, under the shelter of her cloaked shoulders and hooded head, put the package of powder in the box, next to the loose candle-socket. Mr. Wilbur had offered to reattach the socket for her — 'I can do it easy,' he had said. She had not decided whether she wanted it mended; there was something obscurely significant about it being broken. The tinderbox from which the fire had come — but good things too, the warmth of winter evenings and her mother's good food. She held it a moment longer, weighing it contemplatively in the palm of her hand, then put it in her pocket and, with a deep sigh, walked on.

Some time later she passed a man bringing in a cartload of potatoes. Outside a shanty, a woman was quickly gathering laundry off a clothes line. A few cattle were grazing in a stump-filled pasture through which flowed a little stream. The elements of the scene were familiar in the sense that Emma had lived all her life in similar surroundings, but these were not her people or her fields. Back there, the horsemen whose arrival had saved her had been galloping somewhere on some emergency of their own and she did not even wonder what it might have been. She pulled the hood up further over her head, drew her hands inside the cloak, and trudged on through the rain, letting her mind range over what she had seen and heard in these two days.

She was still bemused by the comfort of the lawyer's house, but she realized that the man himself had not really been as helpful as she had hoped. Like all the other grownups — for the moment Emma separated herself from them — he had seen nothing to fear in Mrs. McPhail. Was it possible that the adult world, the city world, contained many Mrs. McPhails and that she herself was foolish to be frightened? And he had not been able to tell Emma anything about Mrs. McPhail's circumstances in York.

Yet she had learned something. She reviewed the details of the will. She grieved at the necessity of selling the farm but saw that there was no alternative; it at least saved John and her from being paupers. And there would be something for them to inherit when they became twenty-one. She would be an heiress, in a small way. She thought briefly of Isaac Bates, but he seemed remote just now and too much like the man on the wagon to be a comforting image. Her mind darted back to Mr. Jameson, who had been a window into another world, not

DARKENING ROAD

comforting but at least interesting.

She went over the events of her whole visit to Dundas. This had been her first glimpse of a town and, from what she had heard, York was much bigger. Would she like to live in such a place?

Into her mind flocked all the good and bad and puzzling impressions. At one moment she thought longingly of the books, then she shrank from the noise and the crowds, from the strange behaviour of the people, from the sense of danger she had had several times. But she had liked the ships at the dock, and the peddler, and Mr. Jameson's house. She tried to imagine living in such a house, having beautiful clothes and sitting by that fire and perhaps drinking store-bought wine and not having to scrub and carry buckets. But she couldn't. She had never even seen elegant women and knew about such a life only from stories. Even being a servant in a house like the lawyer's was unimaginable.

Bewildered, her mind moved back — or forward — to a future with Isaac Bates. That at least was a prospect she could picture. She knew about living in a one-room shanty, milking and tending the livestock, helping to clear land, making bread and soap. But all that was beginning to look strange after what she had seen in Dundas.

Eventually her mind stopped thinking at all. Laboriously and slowly she covered the miles, through the steady rain, over a road that had become a mere succession of muddy ruts and puddles and streams of liquid mire. She tripped over a partly submerged stump; a shot of pain went up one of her legs, which till then had been almost numb. She stood still for a moment, wondering whether the ankle was sprained and what she would do then, but, finding that the foot would bear her weight, she went on. She pulled the cloak still closer to her but it was soaked through and gave no comfort.

When she reached Waterdown, she looked longingly at the smoking chimneys and thought of food and something hot to drink. But she knew no one in Waterdown. She had no idea of the time. A passing cart splashed her but she paid no attention to such a minor annoyance.

Beyond Waterdown and Bakersville she entered the thicker woods, and here it was more than half dark. A deer flicked past her and she gazed after it, briefly distracted by its beauty, but she was alarmed by a snake which slid across her path.

Some crows flew over and settled on a naked branch where they cawed drearily. She passed slowly under them and, very gradually, left the noise behind.

The muddy patches in the swamp were now pools of sinister-looking water. She had heard stories of wagons being lost in bogs and swamps over Beverley way and proceeded with great care. Once, as she was walking along a fallen treetrunk, her foot slipped and splashed into the water below. She squatted for a moment, tears springing to her eyes at the renewed pain in both her legs, then pulled herself up and went on, glad when she eventually reached the higher ground where oaks and beeches grew.

She was now perceptibly approaching home. The rain had brought down some autumn-coloured leaves, which lay on the ground with a subdued brightness. Where the road was grassy and weedy, the walking was easier. But she could go no faster. It was a matter of putting one foot ahead of the other, consciously and obstinately, while her muscles pulled and her feet cried out with the pain.

At last she crossed the familiar stream and then, soon after, turned in at the Wilburs' gate. A candle burned in Granny's room; Emma was a little cheered at the thought of being near Granny again, and then disheartened at the realization that that meant also being near Mrs. McPhail.

She walked into the kitchen and sat down on the settle. Only Mrs. Wilbur was there.

'Goodness, Emma, you're soaking wet.'

'It's raining.'

'Well, it's nice that you're in time for supper. Best go upstairs and change . . . .'

'I can't walk another step,' Emma said without lifting her head.

That awoke Mrs. Wilbur's motherliness. She tipped Emma's hood back to have a look at the girl's face, then went to fetch Emma's nightgown and a shawl. As they had the kitchen to themselves, she helped Emma change by the fire and gave her some hot soup from the simmering kettle.

'Here's Granny's powder,' Emma said, reaching into the pocket of the discarded dress and taking the medicine out of the tinderbox. 'I'll go and see her tomorrow.'

When Mr. Wilbur came in he carried her upstairs and Mrs. Wilbur bandaged her blistered and bleeding feet and brought hot stones to warm them.

But Emma did not sleep soon or well. Her head was full of strange and disturbing images, and the forest itself seemed to stretch out hands to clutch her fast. Only when daylight began did she sleep properly, and she never heard the other children dress and go downstairs. The usual Wilbur breakfast racket was not subdued but she slept straight through it and did not wake until much later.

CHAPTER NINE

When Emma woke, she stayed in bed for a few minutes instead of rising immediately. Her body ached dreadfully and she would have been happy to lie abed and be looked after. But she was not sick and, with a guest in the house, Mrs. Wilbur already had enough to do. She, Emma, had better be grateful for having been allowed to sleep in and ought now to get up and do her work.

Someone had seen to it that the dress she had worn on the trip was dry; she could see it hanging on a peg against the wall. But with her feet in such a state she'd never get into either her own old boots or the ones she had worn to Dundas. For a few days, she'd have to make do with a pair of Indian slippers. In most pioneer houses, slippers were a rarity, but the Wilburs had several pairs. One winter about five years ago they had given shelter to an elderly Indian woman who had come one cold day alone to the door. She slept, by her own wish, in the hay loft, but she spent most of the day in the corner of the kitchen, sitting on the bed which at that time stood there. She was not very good at ordinary housework but, to indicate her gratitude, had made things for the Wilburs, among them half a dozen pairs of moccasins in assorted sizes. The ragged remains of a couple of pairs, patched and resoled by Jake Wilbur, still served whomever they happened to fit. Emma, when she was dressed, found the largest pair of the moccasins under the bed, put them on over the bandages on her feet, and went partway down the staircase.

There she paused, trying to guess by the noises who was where. The door at the foot of the stairs was closed but through it came the sound of Mrs. Wilbur's voice. It paused, and Mrs. McPhail said a word or two.

Emma wanted to avoid Mrs. McPhail until she had talked to Granny. Picturing the kitchen to herself, she thought that Mrs. McPhail was probably sitting by the fire — the weather was wet and chilly — and therefore around the corner and out of sight of the staircase. Emma need only take two steps from the foot of the stairs into the bedroom of Mr. and Mrs. Wilbur and could then reach Granny unseen.

Just then the dog began barking violently and under the cover of that noise Emma opened the door at the foot of the stairs and slipped along to Granny's room.

'My dear child,' said the old lady, holding out her arms.

Emma embraced her, then sat on the edge of the bed, still holding one of the bony hands. 'How are you, Granny? How have you been?'

'Missed you, Emma. How was your journey?'

Emma laughed. 'There's so much to tell. I'm sore all over from the walking. Did they give you the powder? I hope it's the right one.'

'Oh, yes, of course it's the right one. I took some last night. But tell me about the lawyer. No, first tell me if you've had any breakfast.'

'No, Mrs. McPhail's in the kitchen. And I wanted to talk to you first.'

'Well, then, here's a cup of tea for you.' She handed Emma a cup which had been standing on her bedside shelf.

'Tea? At this hour? Real tea?' The Wilburs drank real tea only intermittently, when they could afford it and when someone had been to a shop where it was available. At other times they drank herb tea made by Isaac Bates' mother.

'Mrs. McPhail likes a cup of tea at this hour. She gave Liza some good Indian tea and indicated plainly that she wanted tea every morning. Can't say I need it myself but I'm sure you can use it. Drink up, drink up, girl, while it's still warm.'

The tea was actually already cold, but Emma drank it gratefully. 'I'm glad she's doing something for Mrs. Wilbur in return for all the work she's causing.'

'She may do something more when she leaves. She don't look like a freeloader to me. Now, then, girl, tell me about the lawyer. Did you find out anything?'

'Well, he told me about the will. That's one sure thing — there really is a will; I saw it. And the lawyer seems to have no doubt that Mrs. McPhail is our aunt.'

'Yes, I figured you weren't too sure of that.'

Emma was silent for a moment, drinking cold milky tea. 'It would have been so easy for someone to come along and *say* she was our aunt, like in the stories Mother used to tell. An . . . an impostor. And she didn't seem like she could be a sister of Father's — even a half-sister.'

'No. I guess that's the difference in their upbringing. But what does the will say?'

Emma repeated the main points of the will.

'A trust,' mused Granny out loud. 'I guess that means keeping the money safe for you.'

'That's what he said. He said, "She can't touch your money." '

'Well, that seems clear enough. What was he *like*, the lawyer?'

Emma described the man and his house, trying to give Granny the same impressions she had had. The old lady lay still and listened, her lips pursed into a bundle of wrinkles.

'Hmphm. Slick as molasses, but the sound of him. But I guess lawyers have to be like that. And he seems to make a lot of money lawyering. I don't know whether that's a good thing or not. But at least he told you a few things.'

'I'm sorry he couldn't tell me more about Mrs. McPhail. You'd think he might have discovered something when he was looking for her.'

'I bet he did find out. He'd have to make sure she was your aunt. But it sounds to me like he decided not to tell.'

Emma frowned. 'Why?'

Granny twitched the wrinkles around one eyebrow. 'Who knows? Maybe it ain't right for a lawyer to tell everything to everybody. But was it worth the trip to find out what he did tell you?'

'Yes, and it was important for me to see a town. I can picture York a little better now.' She frowned again. 'I'm still not sure I'd like it. But I might when I got used to it. In a town there's so much to see and hear — something different every instant, some of it pleasant and some not. I couldn't absorb it all, or sort it out.'

Then she told about sleeping in the open, making a joke of it, but Granny was vexed. 'You didn't ought to have done that. You might have caught your death — never mind being hurt by wild animals and that. What about them names I gave you?'

Before she could even begin to explain, Emma found herself on the edge of tears. The scolding went near to spoiling what was good about the trip to Dundas.

'There, there, my dear. It don't matter. I shouldn't have spoke sharp to you.'

'It's just that I'm so tired and confused — and I didn't find out what I really wanted to know — and my feet hurt.'

'Are they still sore?'

'Oh, yes. I guess I ought to take off the bandages and have a look at them. They were all over blisters at first, but of course the blisters broke and bled . . . .'

'Get Liza to look at them again. But about spending the night out of doors — didn't you go to even *one* of the ladies?'

Emma explained. 'I didn't have any money left,' she said. 'Your powder cost tuppence.'

'Tuppence! You mean you paid . . . ?'

'I'm sorry, Granny,' Emma said, feeling again the humiliation of standing at Mr. Lesslie's counter and not knowing whether she was being fooled into paying too much. It was horrible to be so helpless and ignorant!

'It was only worth a penny,' Granny muttered angrily, tapping with one long finger the packet lying on her bedside shelf.

'I . . . I didn't exactly know, Granny. The man didn't say anything and he looked so . . . so . . . I don't know what, when I put down the first penny, that I added the other one. And there was the cookie that he'd given me when I fainted.'

'Well, well, Emma, there's no harm done.'

Emma went on to tell about her meeting with the peddler, but for some reason she did not say much about the man with the loud laugh. She said only that a farmer with a wagon had given her a short ride. 'And then it started to rain. I guess your cloak will dry, Granny, but I'm afraid the boots you lent me are ruined. I was too tired to care.'

'Never mind, girl. I won't be needing them no more, and I guess they didn't fit you any too good.'

Emma looked down ruefully at her bandaged feet in the moccasins. 'No. They weren't very comfortable for walking. Next time I have to take a long walk I'll pay a visit to the Indians first.' Then she sighed and stood up. 'I'd better go and see Mrs. McPhail. She might be offended else. Can I fetch you anything, Granny?'

'Not just now, my dear. It'll be dinner-time soon.'

Emma walked slowly back to the kitchen. She paused in the doorway and looked around, feeling as though she had been away for a very long time. And yet, in the dairy corner, there still stood the crock of fermenting grapes covered by a cloth, where she herself had put them a few days ago — the grapes she had been picking when Mrs. McPhail arrived. It was time the contents of the crock were strained — and that was only one of the chores awaiting her.

Mrs. McPhail was working on her embroidery. Without looking up, she spoke. 'Good morning, Emma,' she said. 'I hope your long sleep has helped you to recover from the journey.'

Did Mrs. McPhail never sleep in? Was she never tired? 'Thank you, ma'am. I hope so too.'

The dish being prepared for dinner was stew. 'Rabbit,' said Mrs. Wilbur to Emma. 'Jake killed a couple of the critturs yesterday. You want somethin' to eat now, Emma, or wait?'

Mary was cutting up carrots for the stew. 'I'll have a carrot now,' Emma said. She would have liked a slice of bread but there probably was none; the Wilburs' wheat had not yet been taken to the grist-mill and there was little flour left.

'Perhaps,' said Mrs. McPhail, laying down her embroidery, 'there is time before dinner for Emma and me to have a short talk. May we use the parlour, Mrs. Wilbur?'

'Sure, go right ahead, ma'am.'

The connecting door between the kitchen and parlour usually stood open, but today for some reason it was closed. The parlour was chilly and damp and smelled of cold ashes. Mrs. McPhail took a chair. Emma sat on the settle, still holding the piece of carrot but suddenly without appetite for it. She tried not to shiver visibly, huddling her lanky, sore body together against the cold.

'Well, Emma, what was the outcome of your talk with the lawyer?'

Emma clenched into stillness at the surprise of it. No one except Granny had known of her visit to the lawyer. Could . . . . ? No, the old lady was perfectly clear in her wits and knew how important it was that the visit to the lawyer should remain secret. Then how . . . . ?

Mrs. McPhail smiled coolly. 'Did you think I was a fool? Did you think that I would not guess why old Mrs. Wilbur was asking me all those questions, especially when you went to Dundas so soon afterwards? Come, child, I won't be trifled with. I am your guardian and I will not stand for any obstructive behaviour. What did you and Mr. Jameson talk about?'

In that instant, Emma pictured Mrs. McPhail in the room where she had seen Mr. Jameson, and she realized how well she would have been able to talk to him. No wonder he had

THE PARLOUR

approved of her. He and Mrs. McPhail were on the same side, and Emma was on the other side. The realization left her desolate and near tears, but weeping would achieve nothing.

'I asked about my father's will, and about you being our guardian, and whether you could sell the farm, and when we'd get our money. I asked . . . about you.'

'And what did he tell you about me?'

'Nothing,' said Emma. 'He didn't seem to know anything.'

The lady smiled again. 'He and I met only once. There is no reason why he should know anything about me, beyond the fact that I am certainly your aunt and therefore your legal guardian and one of your father's heirs. You were perhaps disappointed to hear that it really was so. I hope that the failure of your little venture will show you the futility of going behind my back.'

Emma waited for more, but Mrs. McPhail seemed to have spoken her last word concerning the visit to the lawyer. Emma glanced up and then down again, aware of a hope rising within her. Mrs. McPhail was, then, not omniscient! She apparently did not guess that to Emma the trip was far from a failure.

Suddenly, in that moment, Emma realized that she might be able to live with Mrs. McPhail and still have a hidden life of her own. When her parents were alive, there had been no need for a private life apart from that which she shared with them. Since their death, her inner life had been dominated by grief and memory, about which there was no need to talk to the adults around her. But now she glimpsed the possibility of a secret life, rather like a secret room which she could furnish with whatever was interesting and precious. She might even, perhaps, be able to use Mrs. McPhail for ends of which that lady was completely unaware. The image was still vague, but it was an intriguing possibility. Emma did not again look up, lest the elation of this new discovery show in her eyes.

Mrs. McPhail was talking. 'I have never had children of my own,' she was saying, 'but I have no doubt that I will be able to raise you and John satisfactorily.'

'Has Isaac Bates been here while I was away, ma'am?'

Mrs. McPhail did not blink at the apparent change of subject. 'Oh, yes, he was here and was introduced to me. He came yesterday. He wishes to buy your late father's livestock — for his own future farm, I understand — and we came to a satisfactory agreement. I thought him quite a promising young backwoodsman.'

'So he is, I believe, ma'am.'

'Now that you've had a chance to ponder, what do you think of his plans for you? — living with his mother for a year and then marrying him?'

'I . . . I should like a few more days to decide, please. There has been so much else on my mind.'

'Naturally. But you will have to decide before I leave this neighbourhood.'

'When will that be, ma'am?'

'I am not certain yet. I will remain here until after the visit of the gentleman from York who is coming to inspect the farm.'

'Is he coming soon?'

'I hope within the next few days. I should like to have the matter settled so that I can return to the city. The cabin in which I'm living is charmingly rustic, but I have no wish to live there when the weather becomes really cold.'

'No, of course, you couldn't. Though we did, five whole years before the house was built.'

The chilly smile came again. 'Yes, I have no doubt. It is because of such living conditions that I have never been able to picture myself as a pioneer.'

'No, it takes something special to be a pioneer.'

Mrs. McPhail gave Emma a sharp look, but the girl was apparently staring at the cold fireplace. 'Of course, you must be remembering your parents,' she said. 'I'm so sorry that I never met your mother. Mr. and Mrs. Wilbur valued both your parents highly — though they seem to think that they might have prospered better in a town than on a bush farm.'

'My parents felt confined in towns.'

'How do you know?'

'They told me. They were always telling us things.'

'I shall also, probably, be telling you things. But most likely it will be to sit up straight and to remember your place.'

'Was there anything else you wanted to talk about, ma'am?' Emma asked quietly.

'Not for the moment, child. I trust, though, that you will be docile and recognize when someone is trying to do the best for you.'

'Thank you, ma'am,' Emma said very politely. 'Now I must see whether Mrs. Wilbur needs me.'

106

'Yes, you may go to Mrs. Wilbur now.'

So even good manners could be used as a shield against Mrs. McPhail! Emma remembered thinking, a few days ago, that Mrs. McPhail's politeness was somehow dangerous — but apparently it was a device that Emma could use too! Secretly elated at this discovery, she went to the kitchen with a lighter step than she had expected the interview to produce.

After a noisy dinner, the kitchen emptied and quietened, leaving only Emma and Mary to clear away the dishes. As she washed, Emma listened to the snap and hiss of the fire and stared out of the window at the wet brown yard. The surroundings were the same, but it was a different Emma who worked here today. It was as though the events of the last few days had pushed her abruptly from childhood to adulthood. In the course of the journey to Dundas she had learned more than she had ever thought possible. She had seen a busy modern town, talked to strangers, conducted business, and borne herself with dignity in her meeting with the impressive Mr. Jameson; she had seen a library and learned something about handling money, and she had pushed on doggedly against pain and exhaustion.

Above all, this morning she had discovered a small crack in Mrs. McPhail's veneer of knowledge, ability, and power — and she had seen a way to use that crack. Perhaps using cracks was a kind of power. If so, Emma herself might have a little of the quality that made Mrs. McPhail so strong. As she scoured a knife, Emma wondered whether it was a good trait or a frightening one.

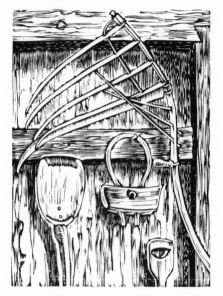

HARVEST TOOLS

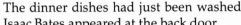

The dinner dishes had just been washed and put away when Isaac Bates appeared at the back door.

'Hello,' he said to Emma.

'Hello, Isaac.'

'Well, then, how did your trip to Dundas go?'

'Oh, it was quite interesting.'

Both of them were very much aware of Bess and Mary, watching and giggling in the background. He frowned in sudden impatience. 'Can you come someplace where we can talk?'

She wondered where they could go, then had an inspiration. 'It'll be warm in the barn. Wait till I get some pattens and a shawl.'

Over her moccasins she slipped on the pattens that would allow her to cross the muddy yard without getting her feet wet, and she put on a shawl of Mrs. Wilbur's that was lying in the kitchen. When she turned to Isaac, she caught again that avid look in his eyes.

'You're looking . . . well, sort of grown-up these days, Emma.'

She gave an embarrassed little laugh and went with him to the barn. In the area where the harness and tools were hung, and near enough to the animals to be warm, was a space where stood a couple of wooden trestles. Mr. Wilbur and the boys were working in another part of the building; here it was quiet. Most of the livestock was still outside but the sheep were indoors because Arnold Bates had reported wolves in the neighbourhood. One of the horses was also in the barn because it had a cough. Mr. Wilbur had been saying during dinner that it was a real autumn day, rainy and raw and cold, and they'd better consider summer over for another year. Hurrying across the yard, and grateful for the barn's warmth, Emma agreed with him.

'This is nice,' Isaac said, looking about at the dim space with its harness on pegs and its tiny cobwebby window and the snuffling of sheep close by. The floor was deep in old straw and bits of undistinguishable but pleasant refuse.

'It isn't elegant,' Emma said, 'but there's nowhere else that's dry and half-warm.' And private, she would have added, except that at the thought of being alone with Isaac she was overcome with shyness. To avoid his eyes she looked at the floor and, with the sole of her patten, scraped designs in the soft, loose litter.

Emma remembered the last time they had talked, when she had been surprised by glimpses of another Isaac, more perceptive and more thoughtful than the ordinary outward man. She wished she knew how to bring out the inner Isaac.

'Have you thought about what I said last time?' he asked abruptly.

'Yes, of course. But I've been awfully busy with other things.'

'I'd be a good husband to you, Emma. Work hard, look after you . . . .'

Once again, Emma felt that there was something missing. In the two or three novels which her father had owned, suitors talked of love and desire. Marriage, as she had seen it in her parents' relationship, had room for more than just survival and procreation. It was hard to define, but . . . .

Perhaps such feelings came after marriage, or when one reached a certain age. And yet, ought there not to be some suggestion of affection during courtship?

For Emma, however, the main issue now was where and in what manner she wanted to live, and how she might best look after John. Living with the Wilburs had been temporary, a stage on the way to something else. Mrs. McPhail's arrival had presented one possibility; Isaac's plan was another.

Emma had been sitting quietly on a trestle, staring at the sheep. She glanced now at Isaac; he was looking at her with that greedy expression. That was not the inner Isaac that she wanted to encourage.

'Well, Emma, how d'you feel about it?'

'Why me, Isaac? There's girls who'd marry you now, without you having to wait a year.'

'You're . . . why, you're something a little different, I guess. You're good on a farm and in a kitchen, but you're also a thinking kind of girl. I can't read books beyond what your father learned me, and I haven't been getting much practice since then, but I'd like my kids to read — and I'd like them to be able to talk about things. I remember you talking to your father. I liked that. We'd buy a book or two, maybe, when we had some money to spare.'

Emma had looked up at the mention of books, but the phrase 'money to spare' was a damper. If she had to wait till there was money to spare on a bush farm, there'd never be any books. Still, she didn't mind being called 'a thinking kind of girl.'

'Well, then, what d'you say?' Isaac asked.

She sighed deeply. 'Give me a couple of days more, please, Isaac. It's not easy, making up my mind.'

'Your aunt'll want you to make up your mind pretty damn quick — about going to the city, I mean, and . . . .'

'Oh, she won't admit that there's any real alternative to that.'

'She knows what I'm suggesting. I made sure she knew.' Isaac's voice was still quiet, but there was a new tension in it. When she looked up at him, he said, 'I want you to stay here, Emma, and marry me a year from now.' He moved to stand in front of her and, grasping her arms, lifted her to her feet. For a moment he searched her face as well as he could in the dusty, cobwebby light, and then he kissed her.

Emma had never before been kissed in that way. For an instant, caught by surprise, she responded to the warmth of his mouth and the strong support of his hands. But then she tried to pull away, turning her face so that his unshaven chin brushed her cheek.

'What's this?' he asked in a soft voice with a hint of threat in it.

All she could think of was that he reminded her of the farmer with the big laugh who had given her a ride yesterday. Isaac's arms were also hairy — the hair was black instead of reddish — and just now he seemed equally frightening. Emma's instinct was to pull free, but she realized that that would be too drastic, too irreversible a move.

'It's too soon,' she said. The courtship had seemed incomplete without a kiss, but she did not really like the kiss when it came. She drew her breath in ragged gasps, trying to quiet the confusion inside her so that she could think. Oh, if only she could have talked to her mother and father!

'Emma, I didn't mean to go no further. What harm is there in a little kiss? Even if you decide not to . . . .'

She looked up at him and he fell silent. She was sorry at that moment and she did not pull away; but when he kissed her again, more firmly, she did break free. The probing tongue, the bristly chin, made her shiver.

'I have to think!' she cried. She glanced back as she opened the barn door; he was looking offended, she thought, and she clutched her shawl and ran through the rain across the yard to the house. On the stoop she paused to catch her breath and collect her wits; she didn't want to be teased by the Wilburs.

Mrs. Wilbur was still busy in the kitchen. She gave Emma an absent-minded glance and went on stirring something in a large bowl.

'It's starting to get dark already,' Emma said in the steadiest voice she could manage.

'That'll be because of the rain. Coming down harder than ever, by the look of it.'

'Yes.'

As Emma was taking off the shawl and pattens, there was a sudden commotion in the yard. There was a splashing as of horses' hooves in the mud; the dog barked and Mr. Wilbur's voice rang out. Emma's mind was still too busy with thoughts of Isaac to pay much attention but Mrs. Wilbur peered out through the small window.

'Man on a horse,' she said. 'Goodness gracious, a gentleman in a cloak and hat! Coming in! Oh, Emma . . . .'

Her wail, half thrilled and half anxious, was interrupted by the door opening and Jake Wilbur ushering the visitor in. Mrs. Wilbur stared, her wits not up to the social dilemma of having such a distinguished gentleman in her kitchen.

''Scuse us using the back door, sir,' Mr. Wilbur was saying. 'There ain't no sense going any further than need be in the rain.'

'Certainly not, my good friend. I'm wet enough already.'

Emma, gathering her wits, knew that either tea or hot-water-and-whiskey would be wanted. The kettle was standing on the hob keeping warm; she hung it on the hook and swung it over the fire, which she built up. When she turned around, she saw Mrs. McPhail standing in the doorway between the kitchen and the parlour.

'Well, Mr. Blackwood, there you are. I'm pleased to see you.'

'How do you do, Mrs. McPhail?'

'Very well, thank you.'

This interchange stilled everyone else in the kitchen, including the boys and Isaac Bates, who were crowding in behind the visitor.

It was Mrs. McPhail who explained. 'Mr. Henry Blackwood is an acquaintance of mine from York. These are Mr. and Mrs. Wilbur and their family. Mr. Blackwood has come to see the Anderson farm, perhaps to buy it.'

'Oh, well, then,' said Mr. Wilbur. 'Let me have that wet cloak, sir, and we'll see about drying it.'

There was much bustle. Mrs. McPhail took her friend to the parlour; Jake Wilbur washed his face and hands, put on a coat, and also went to the parlour. He came back a moment later to say that Mrs. McPhail would have tea but Mr. Blackwood whiskey — 'to take the wet out of him.'

'And what we're going to give them to eat, with no cookies nor cake nor nothing in the house, I don't know!' Mrs. Wilbur lamented, though not loudly enough to be heard in the parlour.

'Is there any bread at all, Mrs. Wilbur?' asked Emma.

'Oh, dear, it's so old and stale . . . .'

'We'll toast it. Here, Mary, come and bring the toasting fork.' Emma sliced some bread very thin, cutting off the crusts and mouldy bits, and started Mary on the job of toasting. They could spread some preserves on it and that would have to do.

'Thank the Lord we got that good store tea, anyhow,' said Mrs. Wilbur.

'Thank Mrs. McPhail, you mean,' Mary commented.

In all the confusion, Isaac had disappeared and Emma thought he must have gone home. But when she finally carried the heavily laden tray into the parlour she found Isaac there, in serious talk with Mr. Blackwood. Emma took Granny a cup of tea with a drop of whiskey in it and then went back to sit in a corner of the parlour, which was by now full and rather warm. Both chairs and the whole settle contained adults, while the children sat on the floor.

Emma's eyes were caught by a rolled-up newspaper which protruded from the pocket of Mr. Blackwood's coat. . . . *ial Ad* . . . was all she could read: probably the *Colonial Advocate*. She hoped that she might have a chance to read it.

Mrs. McPhail had obviously also noticed the paper; Emma saw that her eyes were fixed on it. A moment later, the lady reached forward and lifted the paper out of her friend's pocket. Mr. Blackwood, noticing the movement, turned his head and glanced at her without interrupting his talk. Mrs. McPhail, instead of looking at the paper as Emma had expect-

CANDLE

ed, rolled it up and held it in her hands, which clutched and loosened rhythmically about it.

Emma, watching all this, was much puzzled. What did Mrs. McPhail want the newspaper for if not for reading? Perhaps she meant to read it later, but in that case might she not have asked Mr. Blackwood for it at a more convenient moment?

She turned her attention to Mr. Blackwood, trying to make out what sort of man this was.

'I tried to rent a gig in your great metropolis of Waterdown,' the newcomer was saying loudly, 'but the worthy innkeeper said he wouldn't have let me have one even if he had it available!' Mr. Blackwood threw up his hands and eyebrows in a great show of amazement. 'Said I'd never get through the mud. But he would rent me a horse.'

'He was right about the roads, of course,' said Mrs. McPhail. 'But roads in York are equally bad in wet weather.'

'Help when you get stuck is, however, easier to find,' he said. 'I see that your village here hasn't got a name, Mr. Wilbur.'

'Not yet, sir. We'll be talking it over this winter, when we have time to think. 'Bout time it did have a name, but you can't just . . . .'

'Quite right, quite right, take your time and do it properly.'

He looked as though he would know best about everything, Emma thought, and his slightly accented voice made him sound overbearing. He was a sturdily built man, almost fat, but vigorous in his movements. He was not quite a gentleman, though clearly he was prosperous and had a certain importance. Looking at him and Mrs. McPhail, both so self-satisfied, Emma longed sharply for her parents. She realized now that they had had a quality that she might not meet often. Perhaps in the city — but, remembering her experience of Dundas, she was not sure about that. Even Mr. Jameson, the rich lawyer, was closer in character and manner to this Mr. Blackwood than to her own father.

Quite soon a candle had to be lit, and that reminded them all of the chores to be done in kitchen and barn. It was certainly too late for Mr. Blackwood to see the Anderson farm, and he would need somewhere to spend the night. There was no room at the Wilburs'.

'We can give you lodging for a night or two,' said Isaac Bates suddenly.

'Why, of course,' said Mrs. Wilbur. 'The gentleman can sleep there.'

'You are not a member of the Wilbur family?' asked Mr. Blackwood of Isaac, raising an eyebrow.

'No, sir. Isaac Bates, sir. I live just a little ways up the road. My mom'n dad'll be glad to put you up.'

It was arranged that Mr. Blackwood would stay and have supper with the Wilburs; Isaac would go home and make preparations for the guest and then return later to fetch him.

The two visitors remained in the parlour; everyone else went to do their work. Emma, milking a cow, was aware of the turmoil of her thoughts and tried to settle them. In the coming days she would need her wits about her. She realized the convenience of being inconspicuously on the sidelines, as she had been just now in the parlour. From the sidelines you could see what others couldn't. Now, with her head leaning against the cow's warm flank and her hands milking automatically, she wondered about Mr. Blackwood and Mrs. McPhail. They were clearly close friends; they had made some prior arrangements about coming here and seeing the farm. But what had that business with the newspaper been about?

And did the newcomer provide any further insight into Mrs. McPhail? Only, perhaps, that she was more sure of herself, and certainly more reserved, than he was. Emma was not as much in awe of Mr. Blackwood, but of course that might be merely because he had no power over her.

At supper the table was fuller than ever. Emma sat across from the visitors, who were side by side, and again watched them carefully. Mrs. McPhail looked complacent, though there was no softening in the cold grey eyes. Mr. Blackwood was surveying everything about him with interest and a good deal of amused condescension. Emma had noticed something odd about his voice and a moment later it was explained when Mrs. McPhail remarked that he was an American.

Mr. Wilbur, who was firmly Loyalist, looked up warily at this. 'American, sir?'

'Oh, I'm settled in Upper Canada for good, now. Living in York suits me just fine. York's going to be a great city one day. A great city, sir.'

'How long since you came from the American states, sir?'

'Must be eight or nine years now. Before you know it, I'll be as British as the rest of you.'

Again, as she had done after Mrs. McPhail's arrival, Emma looked for John's reaction to the newcomer. He was sitting beside Mr. Blackwood, eating composedly and, again, behaving better for the moment than the Wilbur boys.

A few minutes later, John spoke out. 'D'you drive a gig in York, sir?'

The man laughed heartily. 'Why, sure I do, son. And on special occasions I drive a big carriage.'

'D'you have your own horses? How many?'

Mrs. McPhail inconspicuously but firmly touched Mr. Blackwood's elbow with her own, as she took it upon herself to answer. 'Mr. Blackwood owns several fine horses, John. But that's a question that boys don't ask older gentlemen. You mustn't be rudely inquisitive.'

John leaned forward and, across Mr. Blackwood's ample front, gave his aunt a perfectly impassive and irreproachable look, then went on eating. Emma wondered whether her little brother's self-assurance was the product of youthful ignorance or of some precocious maturity. Whichever it was, somehow she was not much worried about him.

Later that evening, when she could escape, Emma went to Granny.

'Well, now, Emma, tell me about this new visitor.'

'I can't quite make him out, Granny. He's well-dressed and laughs a lot, but he's not really a cheerful person. He was very upset at being so wet this afternoon — as though we had turned on the rain on purpose. He looks sort of like a gentleman but he isn't one, and he's said nothing about his occupation in York.'

'He's not going to live on your . . . your old farm, then.'

'Oh, no, I'm sure he won't. Granny, what is speculation?'

'That's when someone buys land just to sell it later for more money.'

Emma frowned. 'Then that's why he wants our farm. He used that word and was going to say something more but Mrs. McPhail interrupted and changed the subject.'

'That could mean the farm'll stay empty a while. But let's hope someone good buys it in the end.'

'Oh, how I wish we lived there still, and that none of this had happened!'

'What I wish for you, my dear, is that that nice young Bates boy would buy the farm and take you there to live, instead of way out in the bush.'

'Isaac Bates? Buy our farm? But he's just taken up a piece of uncleared land.'

'I've been lying here trying to figure out, if I was God, how I'd arrange your life for you.' She gave the chuckle that bounced up her backbone, but there was something both serious and wistful in her eyes. Emma took one of the gaunt hands, and the old lady went on. 'I'd like for you to stay in the country. It don't seem to me like the city would suit you, not really. But it'd be a rotten shame for you to spend all your life and energy and . . . *joy* working on a bush farm, slaving to make a few potatoes grow and making do with next to nothing, having a baby every year. But I don't have no objections to the Bates boy — comes from good parents and'll look after you as well's he can. You ain't got the body for bush-farming — bush people need to be short and strong and enduring, and you're too tall and nervy. But you'd do well enough on a farm that was cleared already, keeping it going and making things nice instead of just barely scraping along.'

Absorbed by the completely new idea of Isaac buying the Anderson farm, Emma hardly listened to the latter part of what Granny said. True enough, he might not have the money right off, but he might be able to manage something, with help from his father, and she brightened at the thought of living here, in the settlement she knew, on the beloved farm itself.

'D'you think I could mention it to him, Granny? Or wouldn't that be right?'

Granny chuckled. 'You'd better mention it, 'cause he'd never think of it himself. If you marry him, you'll be the thinking one in the family. Though he's no fool about the things he knows. Living there, you'd still have a baby every year, o'course, but you wouldn't need to do all the heavy work outdoors, clearing land and all.'

'I'll talk to him.'

'Go easy when you do, though, Emma.' Granny suddenly looked worried. 'He's . . . . Never mind, just go easy.'

'Oh, of course I will. I'll be very tactful.'

On the following day, Mr. Blackwood was to see the farm. The weather was slightly warmer and the rain had stopped, but there was a damp haze over the land and everything was still saturated.

Mrs. McPhail appeared at the Wilbur house for breakfast wearing a riding-habit: sturdy skirt, jacket, and beautiful riding boots. Emma, who seemed to be the only one to notice, looked at her aunt's face.

'I'm joining Mr. Blackwood in the inspection of your late father's farm, Emma.'

Mrs. Wilbur, busy at the fire, said, 'Oh, no, ma'am, it's far too wet.'

Mrs. McPhail didn't even glance in her direction but turned to Mr. Wilbur, already sitting at the table waiting for his breakfast. 'You're going to lead our party, I know, Mr. Wilbur. Have you a horse for me to ride?'

'Not a horse as you'd be likely to choose for yourself, ma'am. We don't keep riding horses. But you and I can ride the two horses that I have, and Mr. Blackwood has his own. I ain't got a sidesaddle for you, though.'

'I can ride perfectly well astride, Mr. Wilbur.'

Emma had been looking tensely from one to the other. 'Can I come too, please, Mr. Wilbur?'

'You, child?' Mrs. McPhail said. 'Why on earth do you want to come?'

'To see . . . well, just to come along. I'll walk. I can keep up. You won't be riding fast if you want to see everything.'

She avoided Mrs. McPhail's eyes and looked at Mr. Wilbur, waiting for his verdict.

'Well, now, lass, it's awful wet out.'

'I'll wear what's sensible. Please.'

'All right, then. If Liza can spare you.'

Mrs. Wilbur gave her consent; she never, if she could avoid it, made decisions which would cause argument.

In the end, both Emma and John accompanied the mounted party, which consisted of Mrs. McPhail, Mr. Wilbur, Mr. Blackwood, and Isaac Bates who had ridden over with his

WICKET GATE

guest out of either courtesy or curiosity or both. The riders ignored the children but did not move at more than walking pace, so Emma and John stayed close behind, hearing snatches of conversation about acres, loam, yield of grain, fencing, and the flow of water in the creek.

The grass and weeds were wet about the children's legs. Emma had tucked her skirt partway into a string around her waist; underneath the skirt she wore an old pair of David Wilbur's trousers. She also had on a dilapidated felt hat and a jacket. All summer she had been wearing a strange assortment of handed-down clothes and longed for a wardrobe of her own.

The misty day pleased her. It fuzzed over the first hints of autumn colour and blunted sounds. Even the ruins of the house and beyond it the pasture fence with its small gate acquired a kind of remote historical dignity from the thick air. The first rise of land, where the grapes grew, was visible but the next, off to the left, with its ragged row of white pines along the top, was mysterious and insubstantial. Emma stopped in her tracks with the sudden pain of memory and the pang caused by the eerie beauty. She remembered, on another such day, going out with her father to find a cow that had strayed, and recalled the intimacy that the weather had produced. He had taken her hand just along here after a quick snake had made her jump, and then, after a few minutes of friendly silence, they had laughed at a squirrel carrying a huge nut and perching on top of one of the stumps in the fence.

'Funny little fellow,' her father had said. 'Getting prepared for winter, just as we are. I've always felt that we were closer to the animal creation than the learned people of the world allow for. We have all the same needs — except perhaps that people need culture as well as food and shelter. Though our human neighbours make do with about as little culture as the cows and sheep they raise.'

'Then maybe culture is just a luxury, Father.'

'It's a necessity for some of us.'

Her reverie was interrupted by a cry from John. 'Come *on*, Emma, we'll be left behind.'

She went on, wading through the rank growth which encumbered her legs with cobwebs and burrs. The riders had stopped at the top of the field, near the grapevines, and were looking back from that vantage point. Their voices were inaudible but they made a picturesque group. Halfway up the slope, John was chasing a groundhog, trying to keep it away from the fence where it could find shelter. Suddenly John gave up; when Emma reached him he slipped his hand into hers.

'I don't want that man to buy the farm, Emma.'

'Don't you? I thought yesterday at supper that you liked him.'

'I don't want anybody to buy it. Can't we keep it? Live here ourselves, just us two?'

Emma thought of Granny's idea about Isaac Bates buying the farm. She would look for a chance to talk to him later today and in the meantime could say nothing to John about it. That arrangement would not be 'just us two,' but it was the closest that was reasonably possible.

'Do you like Isaac Bates?' she asked John.

'I guess so. Do you?' When she did not answer, he again demanded, 'Do you?'

'He wants me to . . . .' she faltered.

'Marry him. I know. I heard. And I'd go with you.'

'Would you like that?'

'It might be all right,' he said. He didn't seem to be especially interested and Emma guessed that he would adapt himself to any future which would or might include horses.

They walked on and soon reached the mounted party; no one was speaking and Emma sensed a strain among the oddly assorted personalities. It suddenly occurred to her that she could begin now to make Isaac see the desirable qualities of the farm. She moved near and patted the nose of his horse.

'Here's where the grapes grow every year,' she said, gesturing at the limp and faded vines. 'You know, what Mother used to make wine from. Mrs. Wilbur and I are using them this year. There were lots and lots. I was picking them the day . . . .' She stopped and glanced at Mrs. McPhail.

Mr. Blackwood, overhearing her, laughed. 'Grapes! You didn't include them among the farm's attractions, Mrs. McPhail.'

'When I spoke to you in York, I was not aware of the grapes.'

'Nevertheless they must go down on the list of special features.' But he was making a joke of it, and Emma was sorry that she had spoken. Isaac had paid no attention at all. A moment later the riders moved off along the top of the field and then into the woods.

'. . . mixture of ash and beech,' Mr. Wilbur was saying, 'and some white pine in places. Cedar, o'course, down by the creek.'

'There's a lot of fallen timber,' Mr. Blackwood said as his horse picked its way over logs and among saplings.

'That's common hereabouts. We haven't got time nor energy for clearing it away.'

Emma followed along, remembering forays with her mother to collect kindling wood. It was one of their activities in late fall, after the harvesting was finished and before the heavy snow came.

The horses stopped and the adults talked. Emma sat down on a log, watching Isaac and wondering how to broach the matter of his buying the farm. She knew nothing about prices of land or about how much money he had or could find. But surely something could be managed if he liked the idea.

The party moved off again. Emma went to John, who was balancing his way along a tree that, in falling, had caught another and was left leaning at an angle. 'You'll fall, John, and hurt yourself. Come on down, now.'

'Aw, I'm all right.'

'John! Come down this instant.'

He turned around with the assistance of a branch and came down, but he took revenge by picking up a sturdy stick and whacking everything with it in a most annoying way.

The group moved further, angling through the woods until they came out on a field which Mr. Anderson had been clearing gradually. The stumps were still in the ground, and there were two great piles of wood gathered for firing. Between the stumps the weeds grew tall and rank; there had been pumpkins planted here during the one year of cultivation, but now the area looked completely derelict.

'Not long ago all the region was like this,' Mr. Wilbur said. 'We lived among stumps and couldn't do no ploughing to speak of because of the roots — just planted in the soil as it was.'

'Pretty primitive,' said Mr. Blackwood with a laugh.

'Oh, we've come quite a ways since then. Except Isaac here, who's taken up land further back in the township and is starting to clear it this fall.' Mr. Wilbur turned to the young man. 'You'll be living among the stumps for a while to come, eh?'

'No longer'n I can help.'

Emma lingered again, letting the riders get ahead. She thought of being married to Isaac and living on the bush farm, which is where they would have to live if he didn't buy this one. Of course the stumps around the shanty would be gone after a few years, but in the beginning it would be just like this. As she gazed over the ugly stretch of land, a destroyed forest which was not yet a cultivated field, her heart failed her. She looked at Mrs. McPhail, erect and composed even though she was riding astride on a heavy work horse. The lady was a symbol of city life and what it could be for the successful. Emma considered Mr. Blackwood, cloaked and hatted and impressive. And then she turned her eyes to Isaac, who was dressed in rough work clothes and was at this moment down off his horse and poking about in the ground to reveal the quality of the soil.

Suddenly, without warning, there was a quarrel. Mr. Blackwood had also dismounted and he and Isaac were facing each other angrily. Mr. Wilbur rode up to them; Mrs. McPhail took the bridle of Mr. Blackwood's horse and spoke a sharp word.

'What do you know about it anyhow?' Isaac Bates shouted.

'I was brought up on a farm, young man,' Mr. Blackwood said firmly but with an edge of contempt in his voice. 'I know useless soil when I see it.'

'It's just sandy, but there's good drainage and with some manure . . . .'

'Oh! You prescribe manure, do you? It's a long way from the barn to here.'

'. . . clear a lane around the corner of the bush.'

'Clearing a lane means still more work, you know.'

'I know all there is to know about work.'

'Goodness me, I was merely suggesting that this field was not terribly valuable. The rest of the property . . . .'

'I'll bet you're not even going to farm it! You're going to let it lie, just like the Clergy and Crown lands, nothing but a deadweight on the rest of us. Well, you can . . . .'

Mr. Wilbur, dismounted, took Isaac Bates' arm in a very firm grip, just in time to prevent him from taking a swing at the visitor.

'Great Heavens, what a radical!' the latter said with a laugh. 'Does William Lyon Mackenzie have a large following here? Such advanced ideas!'

Emma herself tensed at the scorn in Mr. Blackwood's voice;

Isaac Bates, restrained from violence by Jake Wilbur's hand and his own common sense, grimaced and clenched his fists. Mrs. McPhail directed her friend's attention elsewhere, and in a moment the risk of actual fighting was over, though the tension remained.

Isaac shook off Jake Wilbur's hold and straightened his coat. 'They're the right ideas anyhow,' he muttered. 'Nothing'll come of this country as long as there's only a handful of people spread out thin to build roads and pay for schools and churches.'

'I must admit,' Mr. Blackwood ways, 'that they manage such things better where I come from, in New England. Villages provide . . . .'

'Yes, that's it!'

'Come, Mr. Blackwood,' said Mrs. McPhail. 'This is achieving nothing. Do you want to ride further, or have you seen enough? Mr. Wilbur, what else is there that we should see?'

'There's another cleared field beyond the creek, ma'am, the other side of the shanty. You can see it from the road.'

Mr. Blackwood mounted his horse. 'How many acres?'

'Four, more or less. That, and the field and pasture near the house, makes about ten acres cleared altogether. Not counting this.'

'I certainly wouldn't count this as a cleared field. How much of the total property is swamp?'

'Not much swamp hereabouts.'

Emma spoke up. 'Just that little bit further down the creek.'

'Oh, yes. But that's not more'n an acre.'

The riders turned back towards the woods. John had run off in pursuit of another groundhog, and Emma lagged behind. Isaac's outburst about idle land and inactive owners lay on her mind. She thought she might be able to make use of it, if only she were clever enough to see how. She had never thought much about it before, but of course the lands reserved for the Crown and the Clergy were empty and their nominal owners contributed nothing to the formation of the community. She understood too how they could hamper the growth of towns — though of course villages did grow up where they could. Waterdown was being built mainly on the Griffin family's large tract of land, parcelled out and sold to people who wanted to build stores and livery stables and mills.

Speculators from the city were just as bad, buying land and

RUFFED GROUSE

leaving it idle until they could sell it at a profit.

If Isaac felt so strongly about it, perhaps she could use that to persuade him to buy this farm, to stay and keep the land in use and to help build up the community.

Instead of following the riders' route through the woods, she cut straight back to the Wilburs' house. She was tired and her legs and feet were soaking wet. Her mind was in a turmoil, trying to think of the best way to approach Isaac. In some ways, she knew, she could express herself better than he could. But he was an experienced farmer and was used to thinking about practical matters. And if he was against it, she'd have small chance of persuading him. But she had to talk to him, and she wanted to do it today, before a deal was made with the man from York.

Isaac was invited to stay and have dinner with the Wilburs. Afterwards Emma had her chance; when he left the house to return home, she put on a shawl and followed him.

'Can I talk to you for a moment, Isaac?'

He looked at her in a way that recalled his kiss yesterday. 'On business, a sort of business,' she added hurriedly.

He gave a wry grin. All through dinner he had been silent, answering curtly when spoken to but clearly resenting the York man. Emma saw that his resentment was not only over the absentee-owner issue; Isaac also visibly envied the other man's clothes of dark-grey broadcloth, his white linen, his well-groomed hair, the quality of his gloves and boots. Mr. Blackwood was less expensively dressed than the Dundas lawyer had been, but all the same it was a quite exceptional outfit for these back regions of the township. She was a little surprised to find that Isaac cared about such things, though this envy agreed well enough with his wish to have his children more cultured than he was; more importantly, Emma had wondered whether Isaac was often so irritated and angry.

'In the barn again?' he asked.

She would have preferred the shed outside the back door because it was nearer to the house, but the shed was very cold and not private. She didn't want to talk to him while her teeth were chattering, and for today's business she did want to see him alone. Without a word, she followed him to the barn.

'Now, what business can you have to talk about?' he asked with a half-smile when they were alone in the little corner between the harness and the sheep.

'This . . . this man from York. I don't much like him.'

'No more do I,' Isaac said with a rough laugh.

'I don't want him to buy our farm.'

'*Your* farm, is it?' he asked.

'It belongs to Mrs. McPhail and John and me right now. I don't like to think of him owning it, even if he doesn't live there. It's a good farm, Isaac,' she said, tackling her task in earnest. 'You know that. Those bottom fields always did well for grain and potatoes; the creek isn't big but it never dries up, and . . . .'

He was looking soberly at her but said nothing so that in her nervousness she talked on. 'Well, think of all that cleared land, ten acres of it, and a barn, and a small cabin all ready to live in, a good cabin with a window and a wood floor and a fireplace. If you . . . .'

Her mind stalled; she did not know how to put her plan into specific words. All she could do was look at him and hope that he could fill in the rest for himself.

'If I . . .' he repeated meditatively. Then he grunted. 'I suppose that all this talk about a cabin ready built and fields cleared is meant for something. What're you trying to say, Emma?'

She had the feeling that he knew but that he was forcing her to put words to it. And she didn't at all like the tone of his voice; he ought to have sounded kinder if the idea appealed to him.

'If you,' she began again, slowly and carefully, 'were to buy our farm, and we were to live there, you wouldn't have to clear land at least to start with, and you could be near your family, and the farm wouldn't be left empty.'

He was silent and she watched his face very closely. He turned away and strode to the end of the space; when he came back he was frowning. His eyes were angry, just as they had been during that morning's quarrel.

'*Buy* a farm?' he said threateningly. 'I've *got* a farm, and I'm damn well going to clear it myself. I got no money and no need for a made farm — I leave such things to them as hasn't got the nerve and muscle to clear their own. What do you think I am, one of them city softies? Can't cut down a tree?'

'There's plenty of clearing to be done still on our farm, and a house to be built, and . . . .'

He sneered. 'And I could just quietly take over and run *your* farm. You'd always call it *your* farm, wouldn't you?'

'It would be a bit mine, if you bought it and married me. And when I come of age I'll have a bit of money, from the sale of the farm. That would help us live nicer . . . .'

'Oh, I see. Bribery, is it? What you'd have is a bit of *my* money. Now I'm to marry a young lady with money, and take over her father's farm, like a sort of labourer . . . .'

'Isaac! You lnow I never meant that. I just thought . . . .'

'I don't give a good goddamn what you thought. I won't do it. I'm making my own farm, and you can do what you like about marrying me. If you marry me you'll work . . . .'

'I'd work anyway. Do you think I'd just sit idle? Do you think my mother sat idle?'

From beyond the sheep pen there came voices; Isaac glanced in that direction and calmed a little, though Emma could see in the cobwebby light that his eyes were still dark and his body clenched. Then abruptly the door opened and Mr. Wilbur came in with a bucket of water.

'Oh!' he said, startled to see them. 'You here? Well, don't let me interrupt.'

'You're not interrupting, Jake.' Isaac walked to the door, then turned back to Emma. 'You heard what I said. It's up to you now. Only let me know soon's you can.' Without waiting for an answer, he went out, leaving Jake Wilbur with his pail in his hand staring after him.

CHAPTER TWELVE

'Well, what's eating him?' Mr. Wilbur asked. 'He's awful touchy today.'

Emma was standing by the cobwebbed window, trying not to cry. She expected Mr. Wilbur to go about his work and leave her to collect her wits in this small, friendly space. Mr. Wilbur did in fact pour the water out of the bucket into the sheep's trough but then he came to stand beside Emma. 'Sorry you got all this trouble, lass. Anything I can do?'

'I don't think so, Mr. Wilbur. But I'm confused.'

'What about?'

'What's going to happen to me?'

'As I see it, either you stay here and in a year or so marry Isaac, or you go with your aunt.'

'I don't want to go and live on a bush farm. It's not the work . . . .'

"Course not. You'd do your share.'

'I mentioned to Isaac that maybe he could buy our farm, across the road here, instead of that York man. But he wouldn't even think about it and just got angry.'

'That was maybe not very smart of you. Isaac's a proud man and it means a lot to him to make his own farm.'

'I guess that's why he got angry.' She looked up at him. 'But making a farm doesn't mean anything to me. I'd like . . . I'd like . . . .'

'What would you like?'

'Books . . . and some nice things like china and tablecloths . . . and time for something besides working and sleeping. If Isaac and I start from the beginning now, we'll be old before there's time and money for those things.'

'You can't be sure of having them in the city either, lass.'

'No, I know. A poor person in the city . . . .' She looked up again, 'Mr. Wilbur, do you think Mrs. McPhail is rich?'

He rubbed his nose. 'I don't know about *rich*, Emma. But there ain't no doubt she's got enough money for comfort. Them riding boots was good leather, and she don't look like she does all her own housework.'

'Do you suppose she inherited her money — having had two husbands — or earned it, or what?'

'Could be anything. Earning, though . . . it ain't easy for a woman to earn that kind of money, except by . . .' He gave her an embarrassed glance. 'She don't look like that sort — not pretty enough — but then I'm no expert.'

Emma had wanted to ask whether Mr. Wilbur thought she should apologize to Isaac, but just then Mary came across the yard calling for her.

'Mother says you're to come and help.'

'All right, I'm coming.'

'Chin up, lass,' Mr. Wilbur said. Emma gave him a grateful look and went to the door; there she paused and after a moment turned around.

'Mr. Wilbur, you know my tinderbox . . . .'

'Sure I do.'

'Well, you said you could fix it, fasten the candle-socket to the lid again. Could you do it one of these days?'

'Glad to, Emma. Just give it to me anytime.' He chuckled. 'Funny thing. Tinderboxes is what I was thinking of this morning when Isaac got so mad. Just like tinder he was, and the York man put in the spark.'

'Yes,' Emma murmured; as she crossed the muddy yard she thought that there was something tindery about her whole situation just now, though she couldn't quite pin down what it was.

In the kitchen, Mrs. Wilbur was grumbling to herself in a way that everyone always ignored. She sent Emma to tidy the parlour. 'The visitors is out — gone for a walk,' she said with the contempt of someone who gets plenty of exercise in the course of a day's work. 'It'd be nice if you tidied the parlour while they're out. See if you can get one of the boys to fetch in some firewood.'

Emma called to John who was in the yard and asked for the firewood, then took off her shawl and went to the parlour. The first thing she did was to open the window. Mr. Blackwood smoked cigars; at first he had protested that he would not think of doing such a thing in a lady's parlour, but Mrs. Wilbur had no idea what he was talking about and asked where else one could smoke a cigar. Since then the room had been perpetually smoky; Emma threw the window wide open and emptied the ashtray into the hottest part of the fire.

She reached around to the side of the fireplace for the small hearth broom, intending to sweep the floor in front of the fire, when her foot pushed against something soft lying in the dark corner between the hearth and the end of the settle. Bending down, she found that it was Mrs. McPhail's maroon-velvet embroidery bag.

Why should it be lying there? When she had last been working on her embroidery, Mrs. McPhail had been sitting in the chair at the other side of the fireplace, and she would surely have put her work down there. Why should she hide it behind the settle? It could have not come there without being deliberately hidden. And no one else would have hidden it; no one dared to play jokes on Mrs. McPhail.

Emma prodded the velvet sides of the bag. Sure enough, there was the embroidery frame and the soft bulk of the fabric being worked on, and the little scissors. But behind was something stiff and hard. A book?

And then Emma remembered the *Colonial Advocate* which had vanished so completely after Mrs. McPhail had taken it from Mr. Blackwood's pocket. The business with Isaac had put it out of Emma's mind.

Her parents had taught her not to meddle with other people's belongings except in the course of ordinary housework. Opening the embroidery bag was not ordinary housework, but Emma did it just the same. The hard object inside *was* the newspaper, folded several times; she spread it out and looked at it.

In earlier years of the paper's publication, as Emma knew from the copies her father had had, the front page had been used for advertisements. In this copy, the front page was solid small print about legal reform. Could there be some legal reform affecting wills or orphans that Mrs. McPhail had wanted to conceal? But the sub-headings mentioned no such thing, and Emma had no time to read the whole text.

She turned the page and found that the advertisements now filled the third page. Just when she was becoming even more puzzled about Mrs. McPhail's wish to conceal the newspaper, her eye was caught.

'MCPHAIL'S HOTEL' said the heading on one of the advertisements. Beside it was a small picture of a building and below that: 'Quiet hotel for ladies and gentlemen in a retired part of the town but close to shops. Attentive service and all comforts

BUTTER CHURN

provided. Meals are prepared with the greatest care and the wine cellars contain liquors, wines, etc. of the finest quality. Charges moderate. Mrs. Harriet McPhail, Prop.'

So *that* was it! All of a sudden Emma could see it. Of course her aunt was a businesswoman, and a hotel was just where you could picture her. 'Attentive service . . . wines of the first quality . . .' It fitted precisely. And that accounted for her air of authority, her assurance, her secretiveness!

Emma had never been in a hotel, but she had read about them and her parents had described how they differed from the small and simple inn in Waterdown. Like almost everything else in large towns, a hotel sounded like an alarming and fascinating place; but however well it might serve ladies and gentlemen, its proprietor was not quite 'gentlefolks.' All the same, Emma gloated over her new knowledge and tucked it away until she could think how to use it.

Mrs. McPhail had succeeded all along in concealing it — and would have done so to the end of her visit had it not been for this. Emma realized now why Mrs. McPhail, when she took the newspaper from Mr. Blackwood's pocket, had rolled it up and not read it. Knowing about the advertisement, she had put the paper away. But here it was again. What luck! — and Emma remembered her aunt saying that luck was what you made it. She could make something of this piece of luck.

Emma looked at the page again, her interest sharpened. There were many requests for domestic servants and workmen of every kind. And not far from the hotel advertisement there was one about a livery stable: 'Mr. Henry Blackwood is pleased to announce that he has acquired, for the convenience of his clientele, a spacious open chariot. As before, he can also offer patrons a choice of gig, buckboard, and coach, as well as the finest saddle horses for ladies and gentleman.'

She had never expected the advertisements in a newspaper to have such direct bearing on her own life. The rest of the page produced nothing significant — though she did notice more requests for domestic help. Could the shortage of servants in York have anything to do with Mrs. McPhail's interest in her orphaned niece and nephew?

Just then John came in. 'It took a while,' he said. 'I had to split some big chunks of wood.'

'Yes,' she said absent-mindedly.

But the sound of the wood being dumped into the woodbox

roused her to alertness. Quickly she closed the door to the kitchen and pulled John, who was brushing sawdust and bits of bark off his clothes, into a corner.

'John,' she whispered tensely, 'I've found out about Mrs. McPhail and that man. From the newspaper. She runs a hotel and he has a livery stable.'

'Is there something special about that?' John asked, looking puzzled.

'It's *information*, don't you see? Something we didn't know before, something they were hiding. Listen, though. I think they may want us as servants. A lot of people are advertising for servants.'

'Well, what's so horrible about that?'

'We're her *relations*, silly. She might not call us servants, but I'll bet we end up carrying firewood and hot water in her hotel, and emptying chamber pots and making beds.'

'I don't want to make beds,' said John calmly, 'but I wouldn't mind working in his livery stable. With horses and everything. I'd like that. After all, I'd be working here if we stayed, or if we went with Isaac, too.'

Emma leaned back and looked at him steadily. He was right, of course, if one discounted the insult to one's dignity as the child of a gentleman. She wondered whether there was any sense in making him aware of that dignity — in making him dissatisfied with what appeared to be his future work.

Of course they need not be servants forever. When they were twenty-one and got their money from the trust . . . .

But still they would be in Mrs. McPhail's hands for years before that. And could the law *really* protect their money from Mrs. McPhail? What could be done if she stole it? How helpless they were, and how ignorant! Was there any way of finding out the amount of each share from the sale of the farm, so that some check could be put on Mrs. McPhail?

A sound from the open window startled her. Up the drive came Mrs. McPhail and Mr. Blackwood, pacing with slow deliberation, her arm through his and his head bent over hers.

'Here they come,' she said and gave John a little push. 'Don't say anything about this to *anyone*, you hear? I'll have a talk with her if I can.'

After John went, she kept still for a moment longer, watching the two with their heads together, and she was afraid. Then she quickly replaced the newspaper in the embroidery bag and pushed the whole thing back behind the end of the settle. She was busy with the tidying when she heard the guests enter the kitchen.

When she was finished in the parlour, Emma went upstairs for a moment's privacy. Sitting down on the bed which she shared with Mary and Bess, and wrapping herself in a quilt because the attic was cold, Emma realized that somehow the decision about the future had been made. She and John would go to York with Mrs. McPhail.

But there were still many difficulties. She wondered whether she could insist that she and John live together — whether she could insist on, or even request, anything. Servants! John was right, of course; you worked in any case, but there was a difference between working on a farm with your parents or husband and working for an autocratic aunt, emptying strangers' bedpans.

She *had* to talk to Mrs. McPhail. But the worst of it was that Mrs. McPhail still treated her as a child. If only she could be considered an adult! Proper clothes would have helped, but she had none. How could she make the right impression on Mrs. McPhail? She twisted her hands together, trying to think. There was no one to help her in the contest against Mrs. McPhail.

Then she remembered the newspaper's long list of requests for servants, and saw the matter in another light. If there was a shortage of maids in York, then she might have a bit of power. She frowned in uncertainty; impossible to be sure until she knew a bit more about life in York. But she might discover herself to be not quite so helpless as she had supposed. And she might meet people in the city who would help or advise her.

* * *

Emma found no chance to talk to Mrs. McPhail that day. It was half-dark by the time she came downstairs, and she had to help prepare supper. After supper all the adults went to the parlour and it was impossible to separate Mrs. McPhail from the company.

But Emma did go to Granny.

'Something's happened,' Granny said as soon as Emma appeared. 'Sit down and tell me about it.'

Emma did. From time to time the old lady nodded. In the erratic candleflame, her face looked more skull-like than ever with its sunken cheeks and eyes, its bony forehead, its pronounced chin.

'Do you think I decided the right thing, Granny?'

The old lady sighed deeply. 'Yes, I guess so. The good Lord only knows what'll come of any of our decisions, but as far as I can tell, I think you're doing the right thing.'

'I'm worried about the money, though, Granny. The money from selling the farm. John's and my shares are supposed to be kept safe, but we'll have to make sure that the sale price is fair.'

'Yes,' said the old lady ruminatively. 'I wish I knew more about law matters. And I wish you were going to Dundas where you'd be near Mr. Jameson. At least you know him. But some official person has to make out all the legal papers for the sale. Make sure you get a copy of them papers. Then you've got some evidence.'

The old woman and the young one looked at each other steadily for what seemed a long while. Emma was mulling over the day's events and the strange ways in which decisions seemed to make themselves. She could not tell what Granny was thinking; her eyes, shadowed by the uneven candlelight and buried in wrinkles, were immeasurably remote and inscrutable. But suddenly the old woman spoke.

'I guess you'll be all right, Emma. I sort of see it. A few days ago you was a child still . . . no, I know you don't like me to say that but it's true. But you've taken . . . you've taken a big jump in life, grown up faster than usual, and I got a feeling you'll be all right.' Her wrinkles smiled; her eyes shone in the midst of them with a dark gleam.

Emma left the chair and went to sit on the edge of the bed. The old lady put both hands in hers and they stayed quietly like that.

'The lawyer, now . . . you need some help with them papers,' Granny said. Her eyelids had dropped a little. Emma looked more closely; the old woman was tired and should perhaps be left alone. Then suddenly the eyes opened again, but they were the eyes of a different person. 'My Bible. You're to have my Bible, Emma.'

'Your Bible?'

'When I go. I've written it all down.'

'But you're not going to . . . you'll be . . . It won't be for a long time yet.' Even as Emma said it, she wondered whether it would be so long. 'Would you like me to read to you?'

'Yes. Read me Psalms.'

Emma settled Granny for the night, then sat down and read Psalms out loud until a soft snore came from the bed. She put out the candle and quietly left the room.

LEAVES IN THE GRASS

The next morning, Emma was awake early and up before anyone else in the house. She had an important task today: to see
Mrs. McPhail alone. After thinking about it, she had decided
that she would try to see her before breakfast. Emma had no
idea at what time Mrs. McPhail usually got up, but she planned to go and wait where she could see when she was stirring.

It was a chilly and hazy autumn morning, the air heavy with
dampness after all the rain, but it looked as though it might be
sunny later. Emma slipped out of the house; her usual morning chores could be done after this more important job. That
was one advantage of Mrs. Wilbur's lax housekeeping. She
took a shawl and walked down the driveway, along the road
those few familiar yards, and into the gate of what used to be
home. The shapes, in the mist, were recognizable still; but the
York man and Mrs. McPhail had spoiled the farm for Emma.
She had been there only once since her aunt had been living in
the shanty, and that was the day when the visitors looked the
place over. Mary Wilbur had been cleaning the cabin for Mrs.
McPhail and one of the boys carried wood and water. So
Emma had not seen how Mrs. McPhail had settled herself.
Certainly the lady never complained about living in the shanty, which surprised Emma a bit because — especially since
reading the advertisement — she thought of Mrs. McPhail as
being used to comfort. But that was part of the lady's adaptability which in itself still made Emma uneasy.

The world was very quiet. A cricket, one of the last voices of
summer, chirped somewhere and a crow cawed in the middle
distance. Some leaves, heavy with the damp, fell from the
trees although there was not a breath of wind to dislodge
them. A chipmunk gave an almost bird-like cheep before rush-
ing high-tailed into a hiding place.

Emma stood by the ruins. This might be her last chance to
commune with everything that symbolized her parents and
the life they had tried to make. And yet she was not sad. It
was as though she had been going through a tunnel these last
weeks, a place of darkness where she could see nothing and
had to feel her way and hope that there were no sudden traps

MORNING CUP

waiting for her. On this tranquil morning, with her new-formed resolution of going to York with Mrs. McPhail and making what she could of what she found there, she could see a little more clearly. The hotel, though she could not picture it in detail, was at least something to fix her mind on, and she felt herself more able to deal with things than she had been.

She lifted her head from contemplation of the ruins to look about. The mist hung over the hill where the grapes grew; closer by, the sumach's red club heads were misted with dew in tiny droplets. The charred beams were still black, but the immediacy of the fire had faded in Emma's mind. Strange to think that only a week or two ago it had seemed so close still. Strange . . . .

When next she glanced at the shanty, a curl of smoke was coming out of the chimney and, as Emma watched, the little curtain was drawn aside. Emma walked through the wet grass and up to the door, where she knocked.

It opened immediately. 'Good morning, Emma!'

'Good morning, Mrs. McPhail. Could I come in and talk to you for a moment?'

Mrs. McPhail stepped back. 'Of course, I was just going to have a cup of tea. I always treat myself to a cup of tea before I go over to the good Wilburs for breakfast. Will you have some?'

'Yes, please.' She dropped the shawl off her shoulders so that it hung just over her back and arms. There was only one chair in the shanty but there was also a three-legged stool near the fire, and Emma sat on that. Mrs. McPhail poured two cups of tea and handed one to Emma. 'There is no sugar or milk, but I prefer it without.'

Emma sipped; it was quite pleasant, though not at all like the tea, even when it was store-bought tea, that the Wilburs drank.

Mrs. McPhail sat down. 'Well, child?'

'Mrs. McPhail, what are your plans for John and me?' It seemed a long time since Mr. Wilbur had tried to get an answer to the same question.

Mrs. McPhail was not a person to show her feelings but there was in her eyes, during the moment's pause before she answered, a curious intentness. Emma watched her steadily, aware that this was an important moment and focussing all her faculties.

'Why, Emma, I will bring you up to be intelligent, well-behaved people, able to . . . .'

'Excuse me, please, ma'am, but do you own a hotel?'

There was the tiniest flash of something in the grey eyes. Again Mrs. McPhail paused before answering, though she did not stop looking at Emma. 'Yes, I do. And a very good hotel it is.'

'Do you intend John and me to work as servants in your hotel?'

'Naturally both of you will be asked to do your share, as I do myself, although I had rather thought that John would be happier with Mr. Blackwood who, as you have no doubt discovered, operates a livery stable.'

'Can it be arranged that he and I stay together, at least live in the same house? He is over young to be alone, and I want to look after him, see that he sleeps enough and that his clothes are clean and mended.'

'That was my plan precisely. Mr. Blackwood and I agreed that you and John ought to live in my house — that is, in the hotel. You will have two adjoining bedrooms. John will eat breakfast with us but his other meals at the livery stable.'

For a moment Emma was daunted to find that it was all settled. Mrs. McPhail's grey eyes were as cool and impenetrable as ever. But Emma met them. She got to her feet, setting her teacup down. She pretended to straighten her skirt but actually rose because she felt at a disadvantage on the low stool.

'I wanted to ask about something else,' she said. 'The money from selling the farm . . . .'

'Mr. Blackwood has not yet made his decision, so far as I know.'

'But the farm will be sold one time or another.'

'I hope so, indeed.'

'And the money is divided among us, a quarter to you and the rest equally between John and me?'

There was again a moment's pause and Mrs. McPhail's eyebrows twitched slightly, but whether this was a gesture of suppressed displeasure or surprise Emma could not tell. The hands in her lap clutched each other. 'Yes, so your father decided. Your money and John's will be kept in a trust until you are twenty-one. But, child, you've no need to concern yourself with it. That is why you have a guardian.'

'I think I should concern myself with it. And I have to look after John.'

Mrs. McPhail's expression chilled noticeably. 'I'm sure you can't mean what you seem to be implying.'

'When the farm is sold,' Emma went on, blushing but holding firmly to the plan that she had worked out during the night, 'I think John and I should each have a paper that says how much was paid for the farm and what our share is. A legal paper. So that later, when we are old enough to get our share . . . .'

Mrs. McPhail contemplated Emma for a moment, then she also got to her feet. Their eyes met. The older woman's face was expressionless but Emma, watching it intently, thought she saw the brain behind the eyes working. Mrs. McPhail was not angry, as Emma had expected she might be; rather she gave the impression of being busy with quick mental sums, as though to correct a wrong total arrived at earlier. A small vertical wrinkle briefly appeared between her eyebrows and vanished again.

'I see that you have a head for business, which will be very useful. When the land is sold, there will of course be a lawyer to arrange matters, and I will make sure that the papers you ask for are drawn up.'

'May I be there when it happens?'

Mrs. McPhail smiled, and for the first time she really seemed to be amused. 'You don't trust me an inch, do you, Emma? I don't know what I've done to deserve your mistrust, but I do realize that I'm a stranger to you still.' She paused and sipped her tea. 'I will make sure that you are there when the papers are drawn up. You will know what the selling price is and will be able yourself to ask the lawyer whether it is a fair price. You will know all the details of the trust and will help me decide how the money will be invested.'

She sat down and gestured Emma back to the stool. 'In return for that, I will make demands on you.'

'What demands?' Emma asked, still alert in every nerve.

But Mrs. McPhail was not to be hurried. She drank the rest of her tea and set the cup on the floor, then clasped her hands in her lap. Emma again wished that she were not sitting on the low stool but could think of no reason for getting up. She sipped some tea without tasting it.

'Tell me, Emma, are you clever at reading and writing and ciphering?'

'I can read and write. I often used to read aloud to Mother

GRANNY'S BOOTS

and Father. I know how to do some ciphering but I didn't have much chance to practise. I can add and subtract, and we were just beginning multiplication when . . . .' She blinked a few times; on no account must she cry now, but she could not finish the sentence.

Mrs. McPhail appeared not to have noticed. 'Adding and subtracting are very important, and I myself will teach you how to multiply and divide. You will be extremely useful, if you write a neat hand.'

Emma was thinking quickly. Surely this sounded like something more than carrying water jugs and emptying bed-pans. Perhaps in time she might be a sort of assistant in the hotel. Her heart rose, but she reined it in with the thought that she must never forget, even for a moment, what sort of person Mrs. McPhail was. This morning Emma had perhaps won something. She would be looking after John but in that, she now realized, she was simply doing willingly what she would otherwise have been compelled to do as a duty. She had gained her point as regarded the sale of the farm and the handling of the money, but Mrs. McPhail was going to respond by using her for the hotel's office work — probably in addition to carrying trays and bedpans. It was the worst foolishness to think that she could really outwit or outmanoeuvre Mrs. McPhail. But it might be possible to deal with her in such a way as to avoid being a complete slave.

Emma found herself unexpectedly tired after this conflict. Clearly it was possible to win a concession here and there from Mrs. McPhail, but only at a cost. With some effort, she rallied. 'Will I have a wage?' she asked. 'I mean, when I'm working for you? Or an allowance?'

'Certainly. I will give you what is fair.'

'I would be glad of some money of my own. Neither John nor I have many clothes — just what the Wilburs could spare, and we ought to leave most of those behind, I suppose.'

'I will see to it that you are suitable outfitted. You must be neat and respectable. We have some elderly guests in the hotel and many people of good name and position. I will tolerate no slovenliness in any of my staff.' She glanced disparagingly at Emma's battered boots and at the sleeves of her dress which came nowhere near her wrists. 'No doubt you will do well enough when you have clothes that fit.'

'And John?'

'We'll provide John with clothes too. Mr. Blackwood will pay him a wage, and I'll persuade him to give something extra at the beginning so that you can see to his outfit.'

'Thank you, Mrs. McPhail.'

'I notice, Emma, that you have never yet called me Aunt Harriet.' Emma blushed and hated herself for blushing. 'No . . . .' she faltered. Mrs. McPhail smiled, and there was a touch of malice in her eyes. 'Perhaps that is just as well, at least in public and in the presence of the hotel guests. When we are together, however, ...'

'I'll try to remember,' Emma said in a voice which didn't promise very much. Something told her that Mrs. McPhail was not really looking for the intimacy of an aunt-niece relationship. Perhaps this was another way of exerting her power.

As they walked across to the Wilburs' house for breakfast, Emma had the feeling that the talk with Mrs. McPhail had been a long one, but when they arrived, the usual morning activity was only just underway. 'Oh, there you are, Emma,' said Liza Wilbur. 'Good morning to you, Mrs. McPhail.'

'Good morning, Mrs. Wilbur. Chilly this morning, but it looks as though it will be fine later.'

Emma drank a cup of lukewarm, cloudy herb tea, gathered up her apron, and went to do the milking. With her head against the warm flanks of the cows, she thought over her talk with Mrs. McPhail. The lady was ready enough to give information now that her secret — or part of it — was discovered. Emma pictured her own future as being one of perpetual watchfulness, of constantly looking for information, and then using it boldly and wisely. The very thought was exhausting. But still the talk had cheered her. It seemed as though she was after all to be something more than a drudge in a hotel — at least so long as she continued to be sharp. Mrs. McPhail liked sharpness: humble submissiveness would simply be humiliated further. For the first time, Emma was catching a faint glimmer of what the coming months and years might be like, and the prospect held some hope. And then she realized, with a further lift of the spirits, that she could learn a great deal from Mrs. McPhail — how to dress, how to live in the city, how to handle business matters.

She began milking the third and last cow, the one who kicked. She always left it to the last, and because of the kicking she set aside the half-full milkpail and took an empty one.

After only three or four squirts of milk, the cow suddenly kicked ferociously and jerked its head around to bunt Emma. Emma gathered up the pail and looked to see what had startled her; Bess Wilbur was upon her before she could get off the stool.

'Emma, Emma, you gotta come! It's Granny!'

'What's the matter?'

'She's gone all horrible. Come quick, we think she wants you.'

'I haven't finished . . . .'

But Bess was dragging Emma by the arm in a frenzy of impatience, and the look on her face persuaded Emma that it was serious. The cow would have to wait. She picked up the half-full pail and went with Bess to the house.

There was no one in the kitchen except Mrs. McPhail, composedly drinking tea. Emma only had time to put down the milkpail before Bess dragged her through the parents' bedroom to Granny's room, at the doorway of which all the Wilburs were gathered.

'Oh, Emma,' said Jake Wilbur. 'Thank goodness.'

'Bess says she's asking for me.'

'She's not asking for no one, poor thing. She can't talk.'

'Not . . . ?'

'Not dead yet, no, but . . . . Go on in.'

Emma found Mrs. Wilbur sitting beside the old lady's bed. At the sight of Granny's face, Emma shuddered in spite of herself. The eyes were open but glassy, and the mouth and part of the face were horribly sagging and twisted. Through the open mouth the tongue could be seen twitching but producing no sounds.

Emma knelt beside the bed, looking from Granny's face up at Mrs. Wilbur's.

'We found her like this,' said the latter, 'when we took in her breakfast. I guess it's another attack, ain't it?'

That was so patently true that Emma said nothing.

'She ought to be dead!' whispered one of the boys in a horrified voice.

'Should we try to give her something to drink?' Emma asked.

'I did but it all come out again,' Mrs. Wilbur said. And indeed the poor old body was heaving for breath in such a laboured way that any liquid might well be rejected or, worse still, go down the wrong way and choke her.

GRAVEYARD

Emma took Granny's hand, which was moving feebly. The old lady's eyes turned towards her but any expression was lost among the wrinkles or twisted out of recognition. Emma was revolted by the glaring eyeballs in the tormented and unrecognizable face. 'Poor thing,' she whispered. 'Why can't she just go quietly?'

Mrs. Wilbur got to her feet, sighing deeply and muttering something about the good Lord and breakfast.

'I don't suppose there's any point in sending for a doctor?' Emma asked.

'All the way to Dundas?' Mrs. Wilbur turned to her husband, who had chased away the children and come into the room himself.

'More sense in having a preacher, looks to me,' he said. 'She can't last long.'

The eyeballs rolled in his direction and he added, 'Sure hope she don't, for her own sake.' The eyes closed as though in obedience but the heavy breathing went on.

Mrs. Wilbur sighed again. 'Someone'll have to stay with her.'

'I'll stay,' said Emma. 'But I forgot. I didn't finish the milking. I was just starting on Dotty . . . .'

Mr. Wilbur put a hand on her shoulder. 'Someone'll see to that. You stay here if you like. She always did find you a comfort.'

He and his wife went out. Emma didn't like to remind Mrs. Wilbur that she hadn't had any breakfast, but in a few minutes Mary came with a cup of tea and a dish of porridge for her. Emma took off her dairy apron and bundled it in a corner, then sat down to eat her breakfast and keep her vigil. After a little, she began reading a Psalm aloud; the old lady's eyelids lifted for a short moment and Emma took that as encouragement.

Later Mrs. Wilbur took over the watch. But Emma was there alone in mid-afternoon when Granny Wilbur died.

READY TO LEAVE

There was no church in the settlement, and even Waterdown had only an itinerant preacher. But it was learned that the preacher would be in Waterdown in two or three days and would come and bury Granny Wilbur.

Fortunately the weather stayed cool. The men made a neat coffin and the women laid out the body.

Granny's will was found written on an empty half-sheet cut out of her Bible. It was properly witnessed and was dated earlier that summer. She had no money or valuables to leave but her simple belongings were carefully bequeathed. Among other bequests was 'to Emma Anderson, my black dress, my cloak, my boots, and my Bible.'

'Won't you hate to wear her old clothes?' Mary Wilbur asked.

'No, why should I? All summer I've been wearing other people's old clothes.'

'But she's dead!'

'She was alive when she wore the clothes.'

Emma was sorry about Granny's death but it was clearly a fortunate thing, both for the old lady herself and for the rest of the family. Emma could not grieve; something in her had hardened and she realized that leaving the Wilburs would now be easier for her; she need not grieve about that either.

The day of the funeral was overcast and windy but not cold. The clouds fled past overhead, and on the ground there were scuds of fallen leaves. Cloaks flapped and hats had to be held on. The coffin was taken to the Wilburs' burial plot, a quiet corner on a small rise of land by the stream, fenced carefully against straying livestock and wild animals.

The preacher raised his voice but Emma hardly listened. Beyond the hole where Granny would lie were, in a row, the four simple crosses marking the graves of her parents and little sisters. Six months ago she had stood here on a grey thawing morning, watching while they were put away. Emma had not cried then and did not cry now. She could not see death as a final severing; these beloved people had moved out of sight but not out of reach or remembrance. They did not really lie here; the unimportant part might stay and decay on this windy little knoll but she carried the essence of them with her wherever she went.

After the ceremony, everybody went to the Wilburs' house for as handsome a meal as could be managed.

Emma wore the clothes left her by Granny Wilbur. They fitted her quite well; Emma was rather tall with the thinness of lanky youth, while Granny had been about the same height and pared to thinness by old age. Several of the people at the funeral gave her wondering looks, but it was Aggie who spoke. 'You look all grown-up, Emma. Goodness! You might be twenty, to look at you.'

All the better, Emma thought, for her dealings with Mrs. McPhail.

The preacher left as soon as the meal was over. He rode off on his sturdy horse, and all the Bateses went home too.

Emma, coming into the parlour to collect used dishes, found Mr. Wilbur talking to the two visitors from York. 'You did ought to be thinking of leaving here,' he said. 'If we have more rain, the roads won't hardly be passable. You got your horse, sir, but the lady and young folk with their things'll have to go on the wagon. Like I said, I'll be glad to drive you to Water-down, but it did ought to be soon.'

'Tomorrow?' asked Mr. Blackwood.

'That'd be fine. Though I don't know when the coach goes through Waterdown to York.'

'We'll find that out when we reach Waterdown. If need be we can take lodging at the inn. I take it that there's no town clerk in Waterdown?'

'No, sir, there ain't.'

'Well, then, my purchase of the farm can be registered with the proper authorities in York.' Mr. Blackwood pushed out his chest and stroked his waistcoat with a self-satisfied air.

Mrs. Wilbur gave Emma an old piece of cloth in which to bundle her belongings and John's. It was a pathetic collection: a change of underwear for each of them, and a nightgown which Emma had made for herself. The shawl which Emma had saved from the fire was now being used by Mrs. Wilbur, and the two nightgowns and one pair of shoes in which Emma and John had fled from the fire were being worn by Mary Wilbur.

Among the underwear lay the tinderbox, repaired by Mr.

Wilbur. Like the memories of her parents, Emma could take that with her. She laid Granny's Bible on top, folded the bundle, and tied the corners firmly.

That evening after supper, Emma walked to the Bates farm. She took leave of Mrs. Bates and the others; outside the house, she saw Isaac.

'I couldn't stay and marry you,' she said quietly. She could not see the expression in his eyes and only wished not to anger him. He had been at the funeral and had paid no particular attention to her.

'Guess I shouldn't have asked you. There's something special about you, but I guess it ain't the right kind of thing for a bush farm.'

She saw his dilemma perhaps better than he did himself. He craved the independence and male satisfaction of making his own farm out of wilderness, but he also wanted 'something special', not realizing that that quality would be starved during the first decade or two of making a farm. For a moment she felt drawn to him again, but she knew that for him the bush farm was the more important. She held out her hand.

'Good-bye, Isaac.'

He took her hand. 'Don't forget us, Emma.'

She walked back through the cool evening. She would have gone to stand for one last time beside the ruins of her parents' house but as she approached she saw, ahead of her, Mrs. McPhail with a lantern crossing the road to the cabin. Emma stood still for a few moments, aware of the importance of this leave-taking. She might return one day to visit her family's graves and Granny Wilbur's. But first she had to turn her life in a different direction, have it shaped by a different prevailing wind.

LIGHTING THE TINDERBOX

MARIANNE BRANDIS fell in love with the English language when, as a child, she arrived in Canada from the Netherlands. In 1970 her novel, *This Spring's Sowing,* was published in England, and in Canada by McClelland & Stewart. *The Tinderbox* is an historical novel for children, set near Dundas, Upper Canada, in the year 1830.

At present Ms. Brandis is a Professor of English at Ryerson Polytechnical Institute in Toronto.